CRITICAL PRAISE FOR *A Good Death:*

"It is a wonderfully simple story told by a writer who shows great acuity in stripping feelings bare...*A Good Death* bears the signature of a truly free voice, the voice of a real writer. Say it. And read it." —LE DEVOIR, Montreal

CRITICAL PRAISE FOR *A Sunday at the Pool in Kigali:*

"A fresco with humanist accents which could easily find a place next to the works of Albert Camus and Graham Greene." —LA PRESSE

"Elegantly written...A moving depiction of love and humanity struggling amid the violence, hatred and ignorance of the Rwandan massacre of 1994, it also serves as a critique of global apathy towards Africa." —GUARDIAN

"When your first novel is compared to the works of Albert Camus, André Malraux and Graham Greene, it's a pretty good start. The book is set in Kigali, the capital of Rwanda, just before the genocide of the Tutsis at the hands of the Hutu-led government. There is a sense of disaster foretold as these men and women, white and black, play out their last days around a hotel swimming pool in a city that will soon become a graveyard. Courtemanche's novel is guided by a strong moral presence: that of the author. He has an astringent personality, and he puts it to good use in this book." —THE GAZETTE

"Courtemanche has written a novel that contains the kind of social criticism that still, almost ten years after the terrible events, is sharp and pertinent...The journalist in him has, thankfully, emptied himself, heart and all, into a love story full of real people that demand to be remembered." —QUILL & QUIRE

"Brilliant, anguished and righteous...There are many unsettling qualities to Courtemanche's extraordinary novel. But above all, it is his insistence on love, and the right to live one's life passionately and well, even in the face of AIDS and the genocide, this double helix of devastating African tragedies, that make this book great." —NATIONAL POST

a good death

GIL COURTEMANCHE

translated by wayne grady

a good death

DOUGLAS & MCINTYRE
Vancouver/Toronto

To France-Isabelle

06 07 08 09 10 5 4 3 2 1

Douglas & McIntyre Ltd.
2323 Quebec Street, Suite 201
Vancouver, British Columbia
Canada V5T 4S7
www.douglas-mcintyre.com

Library and Archives Canada Cataloguing in Publication
Courtemanche, Gil
[Belle mort. English]
A good death / Gil Courtemanche ; translated by Wayne Grady.
Translation of: Une belle mort.
ISBN-13: 978-1-55365-215-1 · ISBN-10: 1-55365-215-0

I. Grady, Wayne II. Title. III. Title: Belle mort. English.
PS8555.O82628B4413 2006 C843'.6 C2006-903304-8

Editing by Mary Schendlinger
Cover and text design by Jessica Sullivan
Cover photograph © Jane Yeomans/Getty Images
Printed and bound in Canada by Friesens
Printed on acid-free paper that is forest friendly
(100% post-consumer recycled paper) and has
been processed chlorine free

We gratefully acknowledge the financial support of the
Canada Council for the Arts and the Department of
Canadian Heritage through the Book Publishing Industry
Development Program (BPIDP) for this translation.

■   ■   ■

TO WRITE A NOVEL IS FUNDAMENTALLY AN ACT OF IMPUDENCE. TO COMB ONE'S HAIR IS ALSO AN ACT OF IMPUDENCE, ESPECIALLY WHEN it's done to try to cover a scar running across the top of one's forehead. But combing one's hair is an act of minor impudence, whereas writing is a more serious affair. We mask reality, we hide our fears, we reinvent things that have been said and, above all, the people who said them. Writing a novel implies a certain perversity. It's not something one can do with a tortoiseshell comb. It is perhaps for that reason that they take away my pen at night. Not, as they pretend, to prevent me from accidentally stabbing myself in the throat with it—but to prevent me from killing anyone else.

Paco Ignatio Taibo II, *We Come Back as Shadows*

MY MOTHER IS SHRINKING. MY FATHER IS GETTING BIGGER. ❡ MOTHER PECKS AT HER FOOD AND SPENDS MORE TIME TALKING THAN eating. My father pretends to be listening to her deluge of chatter, but he isn't really following the conversation. He's stuffing his face, shovelling down his food like an ogre, not uttering a word. It occurs to me that my mother began shrinking when she had to do all the talking, whereas my father began swelling up when Parkinson's stopped his tongue with his words still resonating in his head. I don't find the thought amusing.

The doctor explained it to me. "It's called rigid Parkinson's, plus there's his recent stroke. I'll spare you the scientific details; let's just say there's been a communication breakdown among his neurons. The brain gives the order to walk, but the neurons don't receive the command in time and so the patient falls down. The patient wants to talk, but his vocal cords and mouth react too late. They don't receive the electric impulses soon enough. He knows

how to walk and talk, he's conscious, he understands everything. But he falls down, or he babbles like a baby, and you
get the feeling he isn't there and doesn't hear you. It's not
that complicated... I forgot to mention, it's a degenerative
disease. You do understand what that means?"

Yes. Thank you, doctor. And does it go on for a long
time? Years. Can anything be done, I mean in terms of
medication? No. We try to control it. Thank you, doctor.

So my father is busily conceiving words, sentences,
whole paragraphs, in his head. He has always spoken in
complete paragraphs. He hears and understands everything
we say, wants to discuss, explain, demolish his children's
arguments, is delighted with the withering riposte he has
thought of, the demonstration he is about to make, but then
he doesn't hear his mouth deliver them. He hears all those
lovely words in his head, but they remain there, clogged
like sewage in a blocked sink. And so he rages, or curses, or
sometimes lowers his head and weeps, or, to pass the time
while the white noise of my mother's words stretches off
into faraway lands, he eats. Sometimes he comes out with
a swear word that strikes the assembled children dumb
and halts my mother's aimless chirping in its tracks, as
the shadow of a hawk frightens a bird. Then back he goes
to his plate, using his knife, which he can still handle well
enough, to make little piles of food and push them onto his
fork, and then shoving the whole thing into his mouth. Bits
of food ooze from the corners of his lips. As he well knows.
He can feel the grease dripping down his chin and onto my

mother's spotless tablecloth. Of course it embarrasses him. He doesn't enjoy behaving like a boor. He's always been proud and haughty, like Caesar in the *Astérix* books. But in the moment between realizing he's drooling and reaching for his napkin, my mother has already taken hers and wiped the gravy from his glistening chin.

Nothing makes sense to him anymore. He has words, he has thoughts, but no one hears them. He knows how to move his feet and hands, but he falls down or drops his glass. And so I sit to his left at every family meal, trying to anticipate his rages and his defeats. I prefer the rages. They tell me that the man I once knew, the man I do not love, still exists.

All his life, with blows from his hands as well as his mouth, my father drilled good manners into us, taught us to say please and thank you, how to hold a knife and fork, keep our backs straight, our elbows off the table. To this day his children obey the basic rules of civility and pass them on to their own children, though I hope with a little more human kindness. We were never a wealthy family, but we were proud, not to say arrogant. Proud of what, I don't know. As for arrogance, it's a virtue and a fault shared by most men of his generation. He wanted us to be better than everyone else, better even than himself, which is saying a lot. This obsession of his with polite behaviour and proper table manners always intrigued me. It couldn't have come from his reading, nor from his own background or my mother's; in her family, as in the neighbourhood in general, elbows were planted firmly on the table, cutlery clattered noisily and meat was held in the mouth like a soother. Now we wipe his lips for him with little delicate, respectful attempts to make him laugh.

I imagine being my father as he is now, with someone wiping my mouth and laughing and explaining that I'm drooling and that I should go to bed and sleep even though I'm not in the least tired, that I can't have dessert because it's too rich and therefore bad for my health. I am my father. I know I'm sick, very sick. I want to kill someone. I'm humiliated. I am not a child. And in any case, even when I was a child I hated it, felt diminished and insulted whenever anyone fluttered a cloth in my face and wiped my chin, cheerily telling me what a filthy little mess I was. What's an old man supposed to think when being old means being treated like a child?

The breadbasket on the table is empty, has been for several seconds. I took the last slice myself. I look to my right and see my father glowering at the absence of bread as though he were the victim of an intolerable injustice. A family without bread on the table. A father without bread. The entire history of human misery in that one accusation: no bread. I sense that he is about to erupt. My mother, however, still worried about his health, mentally tallies the number of slices of bread he's already eaten. She shrinks. She looks to her right and gets an approving nod from one of my sisters, the calorie counter. Would you like some more bread, Dad? He looks at me and makes a noise that could be yes but sounds more like the blissful sigh of a baby who has just felt his mother's nipple moisten with milk. My mother looks down at the table. My sister shoots daggers at me with her eyes. When he sees the refilled breadbasket he coos. I'm not kidding. He takes a thick slice, slathers it with butter and pâté, to which he has pointed with his knife and which I have passed to him, and he swallows the whole thing in three mouthfuls, almost without chewing. Rigid Parkinson's, it seems, hasn't affected his taste for bread—the neurons still respond to a whiff of pâté. My sister mutters something inaudible. Grumbling at me, in other words. My mother eyes his gluttonous contentment, shrugs her shoulders and lets them drop closer to the table, so that her nose is almost touching her empty plate, as though she were trying to shrink even further.

My father chews more bread, this time a slice he has soaked in salad dressing, having finished off the pâté. He cuts himself a wedge of Camembert and stuffs it into his mouth with the bread. He doesn't look up. He stares down at the table, his eyelids half-closed like the shutters of an old, dilapidated house. Good God, he's feeling guilty! At least that is what it looks like. Unless he's merely resting, gathering forces for a fresh assault on the food. But since his stroke and the Parkinson's, since his legs stopped taking orders from his brain, since whatever it is that issues from his mouth is no longer speech, since he has had to be taken care of, a man who has never cared for anyone in his life, since he stopped being a man, a real man, a man who stomps around and orders people about, he has been making little guilty-child faces every time he sneaks a slice of bread, and his eyes gleam like those of a thief when he finishes off more cheese in two mouthfuls than everyone else at the table combined. My mother shrinks a little more whenever she sees him ignoring his doctor's warnings. By eating so much, my sick father is killing my healthy mother.

I find myself thinking, and it's not an appropriate thought, this being Christmas Eve, but as I watch my mother transform into a fragile butterfly and my father into a wild, gurgitating boar, I cannot stop myself from thinking about their deaths. The way they comport themselves at the table, their attitude to food, forces the thought of their deaths upon me. There's my mother, who takes little nibbles from the end of her fork and chews them methodically, taking no pleasure from them. And then there's my father, shovelling the food down in gargantuan mouthfuls and then, on the off chance that his mouth will feel neglected for even a second, cramming in huge chunks of bread as soon as the first half-chewed mass begins its descent into his stomach. Of course I have to accept his death, since it is so obviously imminent; I'm not being morbid thinking about it. But when I see how my mother frowns as she talks while my father, majestically silent, picks up his plate in his trembling hands, causing such anxiety among the children that they all look down at the table so as not to have to witness the impending crash, I imagine both their deaths.

My mother will slip away with such a self-effacing expiration of breath not even her sheets will be disturbed. She hates to be a bother to anyone and would be surprised to see so many tearful faces beside her coffin. My father will go with a roar, a kind of explosion, in a burst of anger and terror. My mother will die quietly, decently, like a lady, having always known that her voyage was written in her file long ago and that the only uncertainty has been the date of departure. My father will rage against life, which he will have failed to conquer only because it betrayed him. With his dying breath he'll say he's hungry, if only to put death off for a few more seconds. And in those final seconds he'll mentally go through every book he's ever read and every conversation he's ever had having to do with eternal life. He'll hedge every bet, beginning with that of Pascal. He'll beg God and Allah to forgive him, look around for any other gods to whom he can appeal, and just before seeing that famous diffuse light supposed by many to illuminate the end of death's tunnel, he'll suddenly remember Julie, his youngest daughter, who at the moment is talking about her mortgage but who, twenty years ago, at a Christmas Eve dinner much like this one, tried to convince him of the reality of reincarnation. In the last split second before dying, he'll decide to believe in reincarnation. With luck Julie won't be there to tell him that those who have lived sinful lives are likely to come back as lizards, or beggars. My mother will die of exhaustion, happy to have finished her work, to have raised her children, in all probability to be meeting with her

God, in whom she still seems sincerely to believe. Death for my father will be a humiliating defeat. Men do not die. Which is why he'll cling so desperately to what he called Julie's "idiocies," although Julie herself hasn't believed in reincarnation since she stopped being eighteen and had two children.

My parents have lived in this house for forty-five years. We fled from the cloying intimacy and clamour of our downtown neighbourhood to this new suburb, which at that time was practically in the country. I remember the silence of that first morning, the sight of a ploughed field thirty metres from the back of our house, a cow doing its business on our property. All too soon, however, the bucolic fields to the south of us became a boulevard, then a strip mall, and finally a hideous excrescence of the city. The three streets to the north were inhabited by the English, who ignored us, which suited us just fine. And beyond them, towards the city we had abandoned, were the Italians, many, many Italians, who went to the same church as we did and baked such wonderful bread.

Since then the suburb has gone the way of the world at large. Haitians now live where the Italians were; Arabs took over the English streets; and Tamils moved in as the Québécois moved out. To my father's great relief, our street was spared these revolutions, except for a Chinese family that speaks to no one, a Haitian who dresses better than the whites, and an Italian Jehovah's Witness who makes terrible wine but has a good heart and a dog that barks too much. My mother enjoys her daily visits to the good-natured halal butchers, and my father despairs on behalf of the entire city to see tall Blacks walking down the street as if they owned the place.

It was a good enough house for its time. Two storeys, red brick, set back from the street on a nice lot, plenty of windows and a sloped roof that gave it a certain noble profile.

To a child of seven, which is what I was when we moved, it was like a small castle. To get to the front door we had to walk three metres along a concrete sidewalk, climb three steps, walk another three metres and then up two more steps.

The door opens into a vestibule—a tiny one, but a vestibule all the same. To the right, stairs lead down to the basement, where since day one there's been a ping-pong table, a supreme luxury in those days. Also in the basement, in a corner near the furnace, is my father's precious workshop. The only time I was ever allowed into it was to get his belt across my backside. Through the vestibule is an arch into a sort of imitation entrance hall, two metres square. On the right, a varnished wooden staircase rises to the four bedrooms on the second floor. To the left, a large double door opens into the living room, which contains my father's stereo, piano, three Renoir reproductions and a more recent acquisition, a Hammond organ. Straight on is the door to the kitchen. This was the only door we used when we came home from school, since the living room was theoretically also off limits.

No sooner had we moved in than my father decided we needed more space. There were already six of us brats and a seventh on the way. He drew up plans for a family room off the kitchen, towards the back of the house. Since that addition, we've followed an unwavering ritual: we take off our boots in the vestibule, hang up our coats in the closet next to the staircase, go into the kitchen to deposit our plates and bottles of wine on the round table, give Mother a peck on the cheek and then continue on into the family room. For decades the living room may as well not have been there, as far as we were concerned. Only my father's impending death has brought it back into use. It is now his bedroom, since he can no longer climb the stairs. His bed has been moved downstairs, and in one corner there is a chair equipped with a motor that would allow him to sit down and stand up unaided if he ever used it, which he obstinately refuses to do.

We have eaten all our meals and held all our holiday reunions in this family room, as though we have agreed to preserve the rest of the house intact. Christmas, New Year's, Easter, Epiphany (ages ago, it seems now), our parents' birthdays, our own and our various spouses' and children's birthdays. We pack the room dozens of times a year, and will continue to do so right up to the end, which is where we very nearly are now. My mother has always wanted us to think of the house as the family home. And so we have.

It must be at least ten o'clock, since the younger ones are becoming fidgety. They finished eating long ago and have been running around the house, banging on the piano, fighting peacefully amongst themselves, shouting up from the basement, terrorizing the cat, who is now hiding behind the furnace in the part of the basement that is still out of bounds. We have called them back to the table for dessert. I look at us all and think of the Last Supper. We all have our assigned places. I don't know what ritual we have been following, but we invariably take the same seats around this long table, which is in fact not a long table but a series of small tables shoved together, one after the other as our tribe has increased in size.

My father presides at the head of this collage of tables. Directly across from him, at the far end of the family room, is the television, which he alone controls with the remote kept jealously by his side. To the left of the TV is the Christmas tree with its gifts, all of which have been hefted and shaken and rattled impatiently by a succession of small hands. My mother sits to his right, as she has done since time immemorial. Centuries, at least. And then, moving around the table in a counter-clockwise direction, there is Géraldine, who is a banker, and her engineer husband, about whom I know nothing even though they've been together for twenty years; then Julie, whose ambition it once was to write tragedies, and her new, silent boyfriend, who at least has an honest smile; then Bernard, the most serious of us, a timid professor of geography, which probably explains why he has never married; then Mireille, a homeopath, a dealer in herbs and therapies, as honest and generous as

St. Francis of Assisi, and her husband, a bureaucrat who has become disillusioned with bureaucracy; then their two well-behaved, exemplary daughters quietly awaiting their presents and their dessert; then my own daughter, who is thirty and still trying to find herself, possibly because I lost her somewhere along the way, and her daughter, my granddaughter, who draws suns with faces; then Lise, a nurse for whom I cannot feel any affection; then Claude, a teacher, and his wife who works for some union or other and is a feminist. And finally Isabelle, whom I am about to marry. Luc is missing. He doesn't believe in family, lives in Vancouver. And also Richard, who died when he was still a child.

That being said, none of us has a Christian name as far as my father is concerned. He has always, since we became adults, identified us by our occupations, by our various lines of work. I am the Actor. Julie, the Tragedienne. Luc is the Businessman, Géraldine the Banker, Bernard the Geographer. Our father doesn't see us as people, only as a set of functions.

My mother tells him he has eaten too much as she sets the yule log on the table, and Lise and Isabelle come from the kitchen with the orange mousse and fruitcake. Claude has brought a plate of Turkish delight, Bernard one of baklava. Dad uses his remote to turn up the volume on the television because Céline Dion is singing "O Holy Night." He doesn't say anything, but he grunts something that sounds vaguely like "Shut up." No one hears him. We are too busy asking who wants cake or mousse or both, and Lise is saying she made the baklava herself from an original Babylonian recipe, not that she's been to Babylon personally but she saw it made on TV by a very nice-looking young man with an Italian name. I'm not listening because I'm talking about Lebanon and Turkish delight, which I ate there once a long time ago. The volume of our voices rises with that of the television. My mother is going on about the mousse, how it has been my favourite dessert since I was two years old, although unnoticed by her I haven't touched orange mousse for years. Louise, usually the quiet one, is asking how it is that there is no more cheese, and has someone forgotten to put out the salad? I turn to my father, who has set the remote down on his plate and is looking at each of us in turn with dull, reptilian eyes. No one looks at him. He is alone. My mother repeats that the doctor prefers that he not have dessert. Lise, the specialist in all matters concerning desserts, begins praising her own yule log. She tells us how difficult it is to make, the special little tricks you need to know, you wouldn't believe how long it takes. She gives us the temperature at which the butter has to be kept, the quality of the flour, which must not be machine-ground. She uses only organic, fair-trade chocolate, and the fruit all comes from local producers. It is not so much a yule log she has given us as a manifesto. Everyone takes a piece. The plates overflow. We offer polite exclamations of ecstasy, because in our family we are not big on out-and-out compliments. Over by the Christmas tree I hear the start of an eloquent disquisition on the virtues of fair trade.

"It's not good for him," my mother says.

I've been watching his right hand slowly close into a fist, first the little finger, then the other three curling into the palm, the thumb arranging itself across the backs of the knuckles and, finally, the other hand coming over to enclose the first, making a tight ball, which he raises above his head. I close my eyes.

"Be . . . quiet . . . I'm . . . hungry!"

Then the sound of his fists pounding on the table, the plate shattering (one of Mother's favourites, someone must have been thinking), and suddenly Céline Dion's crystal-clear voice pervading the room with its practised tremolos. He seems more surprised by his outbreak than we are; enormous tears look for a southerly route down his deeply ravined face. He stands up shakily, tries to pick up the pieces of the broken plate, but leaning over, he forgets to steady himself on the table or the chair, forgets he has Parkinson's and that his neurons are not communicating with one another quickly enough, and falls heavily to the floor. One of my sisters shouts at him to stop being so foolish. I think it's the Banker. She recognizes foolishness when she sees it, being so free of it herself. Silence falls over the room, a deathly silence, as we all hurry to help him. But he is already back on his feet, having been helped up by Julie. My mother comes to his defence, explaining that his emotions are too strong for him, he can't bear them. My God, I think, how she loves him! She is shaking, shrinking a little more. "Would you like some dessert?" Julie asks him, and he sits back in his chair shamefaced, his head down and his shoulders hunched, like a child waiting for the punishment he knows he deserves. Then, still like a child, but this time a younger one, one who has been forgiven, he smiles at his unexpected victory. *Yes.* Mother makes a sign with her fingers: just a small piece. Lise makes up a huge plate with one piece of each kind of dessert, as much as all of our servings put together. He looks at the plate as though it were a Christmas tree surrounded by presents he's not allowed to touch. For a while he just stares at it, a prisoner standing at the suddenly opened door of his cell, blinded by the sun, paralyzed by the rush of light and colour, overwhelmed by the caloric enormity of the thing placed before him. Then I see by his eyes that he wants to say something. He opens his mouth slowly and, no, lowers his eyes again and stares at the overflowing plate of forbidden fruit, astonished by the sudden good fortune that has been granted him. The rigid Parkinson's emits a thin th... ank... you, and he smiles like an overfed baby about to burp up its milk.

Before he was betrayed by his own heart and neurons, I never saw my father at a loss for words or discountenanced in any way. It was not a part of his nature. Nothing took him by surprise. He seemed to know and understand everything. One day, when we were walking along a hiking trail, he picked up a small stone, a nondescript bit of grey rock of absolutely no interest to a child my age. This is the oldest rock in the world, he said, a piece of the Canadian Shield; it has survived the Ice Ages, the dinosaurs, Lake

Iroquois. He spoke of that rock as though he knew it intimately. How could he have known so much about the secret life of a rock, a man who sold Bambi bread and pastries for a living, who had no college education, who dressed like a bum when he went out shopping or even to church?

In those days, which seem far off to me now, people put on a clean shirt and even a tie to go to Steinberg's, that temple of modern grocery retailing, for a box of Shreddies, a jar of Cheez Whiz and a pound of hamburger. Not him. He shuffled in wearing sandals that tinkled absurdly when he walked, shorts that were too large for him and accentuated his skinny, hairy legs. Worst of all, he never shaved on Saturdays. As far as he was concerned, going shopping on his day off was not the same as going out; it wasn't a big deal—it was just something that got in the way of his renovating or gardening. So while he walked up and down the supermarket aisles wearing what he wore when he was renovating or gardening, I followed distantly behind him, overwhelmed by mortification.

Now he's trying to spear a mouthful of orange mousse with his fork. Orange mousse is not something that can be easily eaten with a fork, but no one has thought to give him a spoon, and rather than complicate his life further he has decided to do without one. A huge glob falls on the tablecloth. He laughs. My mother lowers her eyes. He looks around the table. No one has noticed. Emboldened, he tries to pick up the glob with his fingers, gets almost none of it but licks his fingers happily anyway. My mother takes her spoon and scoops the rest back onto his plate. He looks around for it on the tablecloth. Then, apparently forgetting that the mousse ever existed, he attacks the baklava with his fork. Not even real baklava, real Greek baklava, the most inspired of baklavas, is easily cut, especially with a fork. It resists cutting. He is too old to be struggling with recalcitrant desserts. He looks down at his plate and discovers the glob of orange mousse that had gone missing a few moments before.

"Ah, good, so you're back!" he says.

I tell him that mousse is my favourite dessert, and my mother, who is listening, puts an enormous serving of it on my plate. My father watches me eat it, laughing. Does he know that I no longer like mousse? And what about my mother, who is explaining that now she uses only 100 per cent pure orange juice and for the past few years has been adding the juice of two lemons? When you were young, she says, I always used frozen orange juice, but you loved it anyway. Funny how things change, isn't it? My father slides his mousse towards me, smiling beatifically. Proud of himself. He wins.

He was also proud of himself when he showed me that piece of rock on the trail. He put it in his pocket and brought it back to the campsite, which meant we were all going to hear a repeat of the story of the world's oldest rock, true or invented, over dinner. When we were older, because he would never let himself be outshone by his own children, whom he was sending to high school and college and university, he boned up on everything that we weren't being taught at school. The planets, stars and galaxies, rocks and minerals, semi-precious stones, the pyramids and Egyptian mythology, the great cathedrals of Europe (which he had never seen), cheese, mushrooms. Even things he couldn't learn from books or by watching television he pronounced upon with such devastating authority that, even if we had learned about them and were aware of the deficiencies of his grasp of a particular subject, we never said a word. At such times it was not his universal knowledge that held us back, it was the absolute certainty of his declarations, and his capacity for anger.

■　　　■　　　■

THE DAY OF THE WORLD'S OLDEST ROCK,
MY FATHER HAD DECIDED WE WERE GOING
TO HAVE FRESH TROUT FOR DINNER, RAINBOW
trout, the fish that gives such a sporting challenge to the
fisherman despite its small size. My mother told him that
if we were going to feed eight people we would have to have
a miraculous catch. What did she mean by that? my father
yelled at her. Did he not know every trout stream and every
forest path in Mont Tremblant Park, just as he knew everything else? But that day the wind must have lost its sense
of direction, or the trees had all changed shape, or the sun
had decided to go off course, at least according to my father,
who for years had magisterially blamed his every failure
either on nature or on the park authorities. Not only were
we unable to find our way back to the campsite, but what
was worse, we hadn't caught a single fish. I had been too
cocky. I had apparently violated every rule of fishing, which,
as everyone knew, was a motionless, silent art. We had
come upon a promising spot, a pool of deep, dark water

surrounded by rocks, a paradisiacal refuge for trout. I admit to showing off my lightfootedness, as well as my ignorance and audacity, by clambering up on the mossiest rock and displacing a few pebbles, which unfortunately plonked into the water. My father was sputtering with fury before I even made my first cast. But high up on that rock, confident in my superiority, I ignored the storm warnings. I was king of the castle. The trout were mine! I made my cast, and in so doing felt myself sliding slowly but surely into the cold, deep pond, in which I splashed about like a clumsy dog, my father calling me every name he could think of as I was sure I was drowning. He pulled me out with one hand and gave me a cuff on the head with the other. I had scared away all the fish. Now we had to find another pool, maybe even another stream. We couldn't possibly go back empty-handed. And so we turned right instead of left, in search of the fish I had sent charging off in all directions. The sun went down as fast as a child sliding off a moss-covered rock, and we found nothing, not a stream, not a lake, not even a path, nothing but forest and more forest, which became denser and darker the longer we walked. I won't repeat all the abuse he hurled at me. He would not admit that we were lost, not even when we heard wolves howling in the darkness through which we were trudging. I was cold and terrified. He swore at me. I cried. He bellowed. I struck off through the under-growth in a different direction than the one taken by my father. Suddenly the trees parted and thinned out, and under my feet I felt the smooth crunch of a beaten path. I had found an old logging road. I yelled and yelled. Suddenly my father was standing before me. He looked down at the road and said, "See, I told you we weren't lost." It didn't occur to me that it was I who had got us out of trouble; my only thought was that I was saved.

Back at the campsite, where everyone was waiting anxiously (my mother and the five little ones, who were bawling from hunger), my father pretended not to understand what the problem was. What was everyone carrying on about? He knew the park like the back of his hand, why were the women making such a fuss? No, André is wrong, we were not lost, you know how upset kids get over nothing, although he did nearly drown himself because he wouldn't listen to me. It was my fault we came back with no fish and had to eat whatever my mother could find for us. Then, while she heated a couple of cans of Cordon Bleu stew on the Coleman stove, he took the rock out of his pocket. That was when my mother and the other children learned about the Canadian Shield and dinosaurs and who knows what else. He could speak passionately about the things that fascinated him. Everything was still evolving, and then came the Ice Ages, and the Tertiary, and the Pliocene, and on and on. Even my mother, who couldn't have cared less about rocks, was caught up in his story, like a snake in a snare. I still wonder if that wasn't how he won her heart, with words, just as he charmed his children with stories of dinosaurs and Lake Iroquois that once covered all of Montreal. Imagine that! Fish swimming up Sainte-Catherine Street! And octopuses and other hideous creatures that later, when the water went down, became cows and pigs and cats. Humiliated, I slid into my sleeping bag and sank deeper into despair when my mother, after kissing my forehead, told me gently but firmly that I should trust him: "He's your father, and he knows everything."

MY FATHER HAS solved the orange mousse problem. A spoon. The mousse vanishes into his mouth, which he opens four times wider than necessary. He reaches for a bottle of wine that is just beyond his grasp. My mother sighs but says nothing. Bernard, watching my father's hand vibrating centimetres from the bottle without moving a finger to help him, wonders aloud if the old man hasn't had enough to drink. There is something indecent about the way children talk about their parents as though they were deaf mutes. They are, after all, the ones who put us here. My mother sighs again and smiles weakly. He has always done whatever he wanted, why would he stop now? I sense more affection in her voice than reproach, but it might also be resignation. She pours a small amount of white wine into his glass, which already has some red in it. Bernard explodes. That's a Puligny-Montrachet 1998, he howls, sixty bucks a bottle, a great wine! My mother apologizes. My father snorts. He's not drinking wine anymore, he's just drinking.

"Never...mind...ha!...ha!...I...like...rosé!"

He nearly chokes laughing. I laugh with him. My mother follows suit like the good team player she is. She laughs out of solidarity. If it's a joke, she's on the right side. If it isn't...

The Geographer stands up. He's had enough. Sacrificing a perfectly good Puligny-Montrachet on the altar of debilitating senility is the last straw. Jean-Maurice, the Banker's husband, likes Bernard and, after fifteen years of ignoring him suddenly wants to get on his good side. My father is now after the yule log. My mother watches him wolf down an entire serving in three mouthfuls and shrinks a little more. I marvel. My father has always been a greedy pig, but never so much as now that the doctors have told him that his greediness will kill him. I envy his lust for life.

Dad, do you remember that time when we were lost in Mont Tremblant Park? I don't ask the question aloud. I think it. His portion of yule log gone, he scans the table for more, his gaze finally alighting on the far end, where more cheese has appeared. Someone is cutting up portions of Camembert and brie, both perfectly runny; there is also Saint-Nectaire, Roquefort and Crottin de Chavignol, not to mention a fougasse that smells deliciously of golden straw and warm milk. We wouldn't be eating cheese at all if we weren't our father's children. When I was seven or eight and the others much younger, he had come home one Sunday and plunked a hunk of something smelly on the table, a small, soft, orangey-coloured substance that bore no resemblance whatsoever to what we in those days called cheese. As far as we knew, cheese came in a jar, like peanut butter, a sort of gooey spread made of melted cheddar, or else in thin, plastic-encased slices. What he'd brought home, he said, was Oka, a great cheese made by Trappist monks in their monastery. He made us taste it. We didn't want to, but gradually, because our father insisted, we educated our taste buds, as it were, and became cheese lovers. And on our cheeseboard, Oka reigned supreme. Even when the American company Kraft bought the cheese works, retired the monks, changed the product in every conceivable way—texture, odour, taste—except that of appearance, we remained faithful to it. We still buy it, if only so we can say, in a rare show of familial unanimity, that the Americans killed our Oka.

Father raises his hand over the table.

"Dad, do you remember when we were lost... and it was me who..."

"*Chee ... ee ... se.*"

He turns to me with the kind of smile normally associated with idiocy, or innocence, or someone on drugs. "Yes... I was... com... plete... ly... lost... ha! ha!" He's gloating. To confess to something in private is like writing something in your will; you don't do it to get at the truth, but to liberate yourself from the burden of having lied. He isn't asking my forgiveness for cuffing me, or for lying, or for the troutless dinner. He is simply confessing and laughing it off. When he tries to stand up, I assume to get at the cheese, which no one has passed to him, the entire family having pretended not to have heard his thunderous call for "Cheese!" he sets his hand down on his plate. He stops, lifts it up, looks at it, sees it smeared with yule log and icing sugar, and licks it clean with his tongue, beginning with the palm and moving along the fingers one at a time, still with that beatific smile which is perhaps not as idiotic as I'd thought. "Lost," he says again, with a nod towards the cheese.

He has won again. Ever since that day of the oldest rock from the Canadian Shield he's known that it was his own pigheadedness that got us lost. Fifty years ago. That story has been told any number of times, usually when someone new was being introduced into the family circle, and each time he defended his own infallibility. And now here he is, with his air of saintly beatitude, confessing to a terrible lie that destroyed my respect for him once and for all, and not only for him but for any kind of authority.

Because my life since then has been a broiling revolt against lying authority. That's what I told my analyst, and he seemed to agree with me. It confirmed his own theories. A dominating, authoritative father, my own inability to direct my rebelliousness against that authority. Finally he explained that my father was a crafty, benevolent dictator and I was afraid that I would never have the strength to challenge him. My analyst did not wear a goatee, swore by neither Lacan nor Freud, played tennis, and refrained from scratching his head during our sessions. He seemed perfectly normal to me, a sort of friend whom I paid to listen to my ramblings. I told him a great deal; our sessions went on at great length. None of them did me any good. But what a good talker I was, a model client! I would dredge up so many telling anecdotes that I must have paid for a whole new kitchen in his house, as well as a few trips to Provence. It lasted right up to the time he made his diagnosis, when he decided to explain my problem to me. He should have kept his mouth shut. You, he said, are a typical Québécois son of a typical Québécois father. He would have gone on to elaborate except that I suddenly had had enough of his uncomfortable couch, reeking as it did of other people's psychoses. If my father and I were typical, then we were neither ill nor marginalized. We were normal, and there is no cure for normalcy. Normalcy isn't a disease, it's a state of being. I'd been going to a shrink for five years in order to rid myself of my father. Tonight I tell myself that if I spent more time with my father I would learn a lot more than I learned in those five onerous years.

All right, I know, I'm wandering a bit. It's Christmas, I'm in love, I'm in a forgiving, compromising mood. Except in my father's case. Compromise yes, but he has to earn my forgiveness. He has to ask for it.

■   ■   ■

BERNARD GIVES ME AN ANGRY LOOK
BECAUSE I'M POURING WINE IN MY FATHER'S
GLASS WITHOUT FIRST CHECKING THE COLOUR.
My father has sat back down slowly (he seems to be moving with so much difficulty that I can't help wondering if
he's in pain). He isn't suffering, though, he's giggling. He
has broken through the cheese barricade. His eyes sparkle,
shine, speak volumes. He sticks a finger in the Camembert
and utters a groan of visceral satisfaction. Ah! ah!, two
onomatopoeic syllables that I take to mean the cheese is at
its peak of ripeness. My mother notes without conviction
that one doesn't stick one's finger in cheese, but she's talking to herself. My father hasn't listened to her for so long it
makes me wonder if he has ever in his life heard a word
she's said. There are those who go through life deaf, just as
there are those who go through it blind. My father is one of
the deaf ones. I take his arm. Since his stroke and his obvious human frailty I find I can touch him, and for the first
time I am in physical contact with him. But when I touch

his arm or his shoulder it's to get a word from him, or to ask a question. To create a sense of security by means of a gentle gesture, as a parent might reassure a child before asking an important question, "Are you pregnant?" for example. In this way I am his superior, for once in my life. If I want to I can become my father's father. I don't want that, but the possibility is there, and I must confess that it pleases me, makes me feel more generous towards him. Let's say I like myself better in the guise of a well-meaning philosopher prince.

"Dad," I say, "that big walleye that won first prize in the fishing contest, why did you say you were the one who caught it?"

He coughs, or perhaps fakes a cough, I can't tell because he's the big boss, a real man's man, as in those old French films. A whiz at manipulation. He takes a crust of bread, smears it with Camembert and adds a pat of butter, stuffs the whole thing in his mouth and, while chewing with his tired jaws, interrupts the operation to knock back half a glass of wine. I stand up. He grabs me by the arm as he used to when I was a child, just above the elbow, and I know he can stick his thumb and index finger right into those folds where the nerves are so sensitive that they scream out when they're squeezed. It isn't the fear of pain that frightens me, it's the memory that engulfs me, and the sense I have that this little reconciliation of ours—and we have to be reconciled sometime before we die—that this small moment of tenderness between us is going to evaporate because of the question I have just put to him. How is it that as children we want to know everything, whereas at sixty we proudly proclaim that life is a mystery? Simply because children do not stop being the children of their parents. There's another easy explanation the shrink never bothered to mention.

He gives a small burp. Afraid that he'll throw up on the table, I take his arm to calm him down. It's an involuntary kindness on my part; I recognize it but have no idea where it comes from. I don't love this man. I don't even like him. My mother gets up and goes into the kitchen to hide. Her refuge. I realize she doesn't want to be a witness to what's going to happen next. She knows the truth but doesn't want to hear it. Knowing it is bad enough.

My father's eyes are those of a fish that has been on the counter too long. He looks at me as though he'd like to strangle me. I know the look. It's his look of anger and inexplicable violence, the look murderers give policemen, an expression of hideous simplicity. I'm no longer afraid of him, but he thinks he can still terrify me. Why don't fathers love their children? Or rather, why do children so rarely know that their fathers love them? These aren't the questions that interest me particularly, although I think they're legitimate ones. I just want to know. Not understand. Know. What do you think, Dad? What about those trout, and that walleye? What if you've never loved anyone? Not even yourself? And what if I'm like you? Like father, like son. I'm terrified of becoming my father. Isabelle is chatting with the teenagers over by the Christmas tree. I drink to steady my nerves.

"That walleye..."

My father has difficulty breathing.

"The... wall... eye... It's... com... pli... cated."

He picks up his plate. It seems he wants to stand up. I hear someone speaking. It's all right, Pops, we'll get it. Don't get up. Someone is being thoughtful. I was going to say "like all girls," but his illness shakes up the categories. We all react the same when he takes his plate and starts to get up. We know him, we know what will happen. He'll probably fall and the plate will break and the cheese will land on the rug. We want to prevent that from happening. My father has always carried his own plate into the kitchen, never anyone else's. He never helped my mother except for that one plate, which is his and therefore his responsibility. All his life he has put his own plate in the sink, turned on the tap, carefully washed it and set it on the counter. He never dried it. Drying dishes was a woman's job. Or a child's. But he always washed his plate. Now we take the plate from him. He doesn't say thank you because we are not doing him a favour. He sighs and looks at me. I look down at my plate and forget about the walleye. Why is he asking me to bear witness to the theft of his plate? It's not as though I've ever even tried to pretend that I harbour any sympathy for him.

What does an old man do who, as death approaches, has it explained to him in incontrovertible, scientific terms that if he wants to live for another few years he has to stop living, move as little as possible, eat things he doesn't like and avoid having strong emotions? How does he react to being told that if he wants to go on living he has to cease being alive? He thumbs his nose at the few extra days such a diet would procure for him. He knows better than anyone that he's going to die anyway.

He lives with his death. He feels it in his limbs, which no longer follow him around; he senses it in his sleep, which refuses to come as he lies on his back staring at shadows he doesn't recognize on the ceiling. How does anyone as proud as him react? Does he bow down and die politely according to the rules, as his doctors and everyone else around him advise him to do? Does he suddenly become compliant, obedient? Sometimes I think that's exactly what we're asking him to do. My father is neither obedient nor polite; he rages against the death that wants to rob him of life. But he knows...

Stubborn as ever, he insists on washing his plate as though his entire life depends on it. But tonight, in the great irritation that is Christmas, such a thing is not permitted. We spare him the gesture. We protect him. Is it really because we want to keep him among us? It's the first time I've asked myself that question. An unfamiliar shame creeps over me. A shame composed of a hundred little lies, a thousand meaningless hellos, the shame of looking at him without actually meeting his eyes; worse, the shame of not saying outright: die, Dad, die if you want to. Do it for us if not for yourself. Give us this one last gift. Die.

I look around for Isabelle. With her I have come to understand what tenderness, respect and, most of all, letting go mean. In a way she's my redemption. The oldest rock of my life.

I don't see her anywhere. She must be in the kitchen, talking to my mother, who will be describing the confusion my father's unpredictability is causing her. Or the exhaustion. Someone at the table explains that my father exaggerates everything, probably just to get on my mother's nerves. Not only does she organize his life as husband, father, provider, but also she has to look after the finances and the upkeep of the house, and prepare all the meals. It's the Homeopath, overflowing with generosity. She doesn't accuse, she merely states, nonjudgemental to the core. She says what she knows she will see. The Geographer agrees and goes a step or two further. Not my brother. He's having none of it. "You'd think he does it on purpose just to piss people off..." My brother has had enough of this life of my father's that won't stop ending. It makes him uneasy. He's not happy with anything that doesn't work the way it's supposed to. Anything that goes unsaid upsets him. He's a technician, he believes in science. Life to him is a machine, complex but decipherable to those in the know. Life shouldn't rebel against the expertise of mechanics, i.e., doctors. And every doctor that my father has seen, without exception, has told him that if he wants to stay alive he must stop eating the way he has always eaten. And so now my father's other son is looking at me, whether scornfully or defiantly I can't tell. "You obviously don't agree," he says. "You never take anything seriously." I never discuss things with him, if that's what he means, or hardly ever. We travel in different galaxies, occasionally, as in *Star*

Wars, sharing the same planet when we must. But we come here for different reasons, he and I. How could I explain to him in a way he would understand that I take everything seriously, and that what shocks him also moves and saddens me?

I see my mother talking to Isabelle, bending her ear, as the saying goes, an ear that rarely reveals what is going on in the head to which it is attached, but into which you can launch yourself as you would down a slide into a deep chasm. My father has finally risen, having shaken off all remonstrations, and is washing his plate at the sink, moving as methodically as a deep-sea diver. I go over to him. He puts the plate on the rack and I pick it up and start to dry it. He turns and looks at me as though I were the detective who has been tailing him all his life and now has him cornered, and it's confession time. Okay, copper, he says, the jig's up.

"The walleye... you... can't..."

He looks down. Why does he always assume the contrite expression of someone who is constantly being accused of something? I could kick myself for having brought up that old memory. It was only because we were talking about the trout we didn't catch. Memory functions like a kind of search engine, and it associated trout with walleye. My mouth, which doesn't always stop to consider what it's saying, did the rest. I certainly don't want him to think I'm hunting him down, harassing him, or that I have some old accounts to settle. That may once have been the case. Today, though, I'm simply motivated by an almost infantile curiosity. "What's your secret, Daddy?" asks the amazed child. "How did you always manage to come out on top?" It amuses me to bring up the past. I'm happy. At last, after so many simulacra of happiness, so many brilliantly or poorly disguised black holes. Those who are happy have no accounts to settle with those who are not. They go back to square one. Their happiness wipes their slates clean.

My mother's face freezes like that of a terrified child. Whatever she was about to say dies on her parted lips. Her eyelids, creased by so many tiny wrinkles, close slowly over eyes filling with tears. It pains her to be seeing what she is seeing. My father turns his back to the sink and looks off into space as Bernard, Lise and Claude come into the kitchen carrying plates and platters. They stop in their tracks and look at one another, wonderingly. My father is crying, and it's not a pretty sight. His whole face has dissolved into tears—eyes, nose, mouth. He sniffs and runs the back of his hand across his nose, which is dripping, and then runs the other hand over his wet mouth. I don't know who it is who says, You're not well, or which one of the sisters, speaking softly, says, He's obviously had too much to drink and eat and he should have listened to the doctors, but of course he never does what anyone tells him to do. Dad, you're being unreasonable! So what? I know he hasn't heard a word anyone has spoken, but it's as though they have been directed at me. I have become my father, I hear what they are saying about my tears, my weakness, no doubt even about these dishes I must have only half-washed. But I tried so hard. I take him firmly by the arm, hold him tightly at the top of his elbow as he held me so often when I was a child, and I draw him towards me.

"Come on, Dad, you should lie down."

"No... the walleye... the presents..."

"We can talk about the walleye tomorrow... Rest for a while, and you can come back later for the presents."

He lets me lead him towards his bed, no longer crying. My mother has opened her eyes again and is trying to recover her party face, while the children (as I call my brothers and sisters, because I'm the eldest) go back to stacking plates and bowls on the round kitchen table. I think it's Claude who makes a joke, wanting to defuse the drama of the situation, and then installs himself at the sink in my father's place to finish the dishes. My father shuffles slowly across the kitchen tiles. I don't like this physical contact I have with him. He's not aware of this. It's far too late to explain to him how distasteful it is for me to be holding him up, walking beside him. And useless. I know what I'm doing, I'm helping an old man to bed, an old man who is dying, and it doesn't matter which old man, or that he reminds me of a dying father. I can live with that.

■   ■   ■

HE'S LYING ON HIS BED, MUTTERING TO HIMSELF. FROM THE KITCHEN I CAN HEAR THE SOUNDS OF CLATTERING DISHES AND HUSHED conversations. He doesn't want to get undressed. I didn't offer to help him, which bothers me. I just watched him lie down on the bed, normally a fairly simple procedure. What could be easier than to let yourself flop down on the bed, or rather, since he is a methodical person, to sit on the edge, take off your shoes and then, in a movement that encompasses the whole operation, let your spine arch back, head hit the pillow, and not even notice your legs as they follow the rest of the body and assume their customary position. In order for him to sit I had to hold him. Then he instinctively bent over to untie his shoes, forgetting that he can no longer do that. He can't bend his back far enough to reach the laces. I offered to undo them for him but the sequence of grunts with which my offer was met I assumed meant no. His body is no longer a whole. Nothing seems attached to anything else, his head to his neck, his hips to his legs, his arms, which dangle at his sides, to his shoulders. He leaned on the bed on one elbow and with his left hand reached down and pulled his left leg up. The other leg followed, but not without some effort. All the motions we normally make without thinking, he has to mentally break up into their component parts, try to put them back together again, then execute them, step by step, so that moving is no longer a graceful dance but a halting, arduous process. I stand here as useless as a coat hook in a garden. His eyes light on the piano and he says the word, piano, then they turn to the Hammond organ and he says, organ. He completes the survey of his horizon by contemplating the small stereo that sits proudly atop an old cabinet that contains his turntable from the 1940s. He does not say, music. I ask him if he wants to listen to a record, or if I can play something for him on the piano or the organ.

"Too... much..." He looks for the word. "Too... much... noise."

"It won't bother anyone."

He shakes his head angrily. He doesn't understand that I don't understand.

"Too... much... for me... noise. The others..."

It suddenly occurs to me that I haven't heard a single note of music in this house for two years. Whenever I've come on my own to visit, there has not been a sound from the piano or the organ or the stereo. It was in this very room, this living room, that I first discovered music, those mysterious sounds wafting out to me from the turntable, sending me off, I have no idea why, into realms of dreaming, crying, dancing, even when I was a small child. As with all autodidacts, my father's taste flitted about everywhere without logic or consistency: Tchaikovsky and Beethoven mostly, Chopin's sonatas, but also Nat King Cole, Liberace, Louis Armstrong, Edith Piaf, Sinatra. And, to remind himself of I don't know what—his worker origins, perhaps—the slushy music of polkas and accordions and military marches. His favourite records of all, however, were Bach's toccatas and fugues as played by Albert Schweitzer, the mythical doctor and modestly talented organist who avowed great love for the African people, whom he thought were so poorly evolved intellectually and to whom he dedicated his life. Father admired Schweitzer a great deal, Africans not so much.

IT WAS ABOUT one in the morning when I was awakened by a violent argument coming from my parents' bedroom, which was on the second floor next to the room I shared with Richard. I could hear my father shouting and my mother crying, pleading with him, then a sudden scream of pain. It was the first time I'd heard a woman scream and it terrified me. I was seven. Then there were loud footsteps, curses ringing out down the stairs, then thunder, a hurricane of noise roaring from the Hammond organ, which, until then, I'd known only to make the light, tinkling sounds of flutes, trumpets or violins. I know now that it was the most famous of Bach's toccatas and fugues. Father had cranked the volume up to full blast, pounding the pedals so hard that the whole house shook, even the walls and floors, under the assault from the heavy vibrations of the music. Richard woke up screaming, and my mother came into our room to tell us not to worry, that our father was just playing some music to calm himself down. Then the doorbell rang and the music stopped. I could hear the neighbour's voice, and of course that of my father: "What? You don't like Johann Sebastian Bach? You don't like great music? You're an idiot!" And the door slamming shut. I was already beginning to realize that in my father's view, there weren't many people in the world who weren't idiots, and I was afraid that I was one myself. He went back to pounding out Bach until the police arrived. After a long, heated discussion, they agreed that Bach was a great musician but that he shouldn't be played at two o'clock in the morning. My father agreed. We went to sleep to the "Moonlight Sonata," our tears dried and our fears put off until another time.

"DO YOU remember Bach's 'Toccata and Fugue'?"

He glares at me as though I'm beginning to get on his nerves. He wants me to leave so he can enjoy the peace and quiet that comes to him only in sleep.

"No... The walleye... I'm... going..."

He gives up, closes his eyes. Which confession was he going to make? The walleye or Bach?

I GO BACK to the kitchen. My mother, who has lived with my father's stormy moods, his highs and sudden lows, for sixty years, has already forgotten his tears—fortunately, for how could she have survived so long if not by lowering the curtain after each little drama? Her days are filled with these outbursts that have us, the children, running for cover. After each holiday we go home. She stays here. And, I imagine, has to pick up the pieces the next morning, delicately but firmly putting all the dots back on all the *i*'s. If she had the same outraged response as we do, it would kill her. I sit down beside her. She gently pats the back of my hand and lets herself be reassured.

"Don't worry about him," she tells me. "He'll be better tomorrow. He drank a bit too much. These family holidays are always hard on him, emotionally."

All right, I'm a ten-year-old. My mother has patted my hand and I'm happy. Why do parents have to die in order for their children to feel grown up? She goes back to her conversation with Isabelle. They're planning our wedding reception. Isabelle and I are getting married next month. The wedding will let my mother die happy, or nearly, knowing that all of her children are happy, or at least being looked after. I'm the last one, and it looked as though being happy and being taken care of were both going to elude me.

"You don't know how happy you two are making me..." She pauses. "But I'm not sure your father and I will be able to go..."

Isabelle protests. I add my exclamations.

"It's too complicated," she adds, implying that we should let her have her way in order to avoid certain problems that no one else has mentioned or even thought about.

a good death

She's afraid that my father will spill wine on the tablecloth during the speeches, or splutter incoherently in front of Isabelle's family. Don't misunderstand me: she's not afraid of being humiliated herself (well, maybe a little, but only a little). She wants to protect my father from embarrassing himself, but mostly she wants to spare him the emotions that the doctor has told her will kill him. She believes she has to save him from what to us is life, so that he won't die. She can't let him have feelings any more than she can let him have saturated fats. She has to prevent him from being happy in order to prolong his life. She doesn't put it that way, but that's how I understand it.

On this subject the family is divided. I hear one of my brothers speaking about the embarrassment my father would cause so many people he doesn't know, especially Isabelle's very respectable family, whom no one but me has met yet, and my actor friends, some of whom are well known and even, in some circles, very well known. Of course they would be embarrassed if the old man suddenly tumbled out of his chair, or dumped his soup on Isabelle's wedding dress. It goes without saying, there's no point in discussing it. We need to face up to the anxiety he could cause, the embarrassment, the mortified smiles he would bring to all our faces. Put it this way: a sick person has certain inalienable rights. He is absolutely free to be a sick person if he wants, as long as he doesn't act like a sick person, like an old man who is dying. If he is to be allowed to exist, a sick person must be in perfect health. Or at least be a polite sick person, one who is capable of hiding the fact that he is dying.

Com... pli... cated, as my father would say. I don't think it is all that complicated, but I understand that no one wants to argue with my mother. Cats scurry off when you approach them directly, and come back only when they feel like it. Birds are worse. Mother is a catbird.

She asks me about my conversation with my father. I try to change the subject, not wanting to upset her and have her scurry off. I tell her we talked about music, that he told me music made too much noise.

Her hand, still resting on mine, trembles faintly and lifts away, joins her other hand, and together they support her delicate head. I realize how easily her head could shatter, how, like fragile porcelain balanced on a pair of alabaster hands, her tiny bird's head could come crashing down onto the table.

"You mustn't talk to him about music, it's too emotional."

She wants me to be grateful that she hasn't chosen other words. Music. Emotion.

I couldn't live without emotions. Without the thrill of worry, or uncertainty, or surprise; without emotion, yes, of course I would die. So are we killing my father by hurling emotions at him? By letting him live? I don't ask that because she's gone back to talking to Isabelle about the wedding dress, which Isabelle is keeping a secret from me so that I'll be the more moved when I see her in it, and I am looking forward to having that emotional response, that leap of eye and heart, that sudden surprise she is preparing for me without asking my advice. She won't even tell me what colour it is.

"My love, at least tell me the colour."

"If I tell you the colour, you'll see the whole dress."

"No, just the colour, colour doesn't tell me anything."

"Colour is everything."

That's emotion, and it makes me want to live.

Mother's hands are still cradling her fragile head.

"The doctor told me he's to avoid strong emotions. They're bad for his heart."

"What about his head? Are they bad for his head? And his happiness? Are they contraindicated for that, too?"

Isabelle looks at me like a mother who wants to slap a child for behaving badly.

AROUND THE FAMILY room the voices have become more muffled. I have the impression that they are calculating and consultative, as if they're in some kind of informal family meeting called to decide the fate of our parents, either tonight or a few weeks down the road, the next time my father falls or when the majority of us, acting out of concern for my mother's health, decide their respective futures for them. Since his stroke, some of us have already been avenging ourselves for his strictness during our childhoods, trying to take over most of the responsibility for the house. It's not meanness or revenge in the literal sense of those words,

I suppose. But I know what we are doing: unconsciously, we are reproducing the models of our respective childhoods. It seems to me that Bernard wants to re-create for our parents the constricting order they imposed on him. The Banker wants to install the logical, predictable organizational system she has at the bank, of which she is vice-president. As far as my father's fate is concerned (and we have discussed it at great length), there are two opposing schools of thought: the Medicals and the Buddhists. The Medicals don't drink, not really. They chart their glycemia, their blood-alcohol levels, the number of calories burned. If they smoke, it's only with their evening coffee, preferably on Friday or Saturday. The Medicals, at least the women, weigh themselves every night. The Buddhists smoke like chimneys or not at all, drink as much as they feel like drinking and have completely contradictory opinions about everything. They're fine with letting my father's life take its normal course, letting him enjoy all the pleasures prohibited by hard-line doctors, but at the same time they wish that the ensuing flood of happiness, enjoyed in the teeth of the medical experts, would also lead to more happiness for my mother. But that's the catch. If my father eats too many oysters and too much foie gras, he'll grunt with satisfaction, but the next morning, when all the Buddhists are home meditating into the rising sun, it's our dear, frail little mother who has to pick him up when he falls down because he blacked out from having stuffed too much fat into the old paternal metabolism. We know absolutely nothing about that. That's where the two schools come up, however cautiously and timidly, against my mother's concern. For us, she is the incarnation of everything we want the life awaiting us to be like. My father's illness has given her back her soul, her voice; with her shining eyes, her arresting smile, her legendary family, the way she is with the Algerian butcher, so open-minded, she is more alive now than she ever was under my father's thumb.

I have to admit, on the other hand, that my father has given us the worst example we could have of growing old. Even before he reached his advanced age he never did anything to endear himself to us, or to intrigue us or give us anything to admire in him. No family stories, no memories, no projects with us. The first time he ever shared a confidence with me was this evening, when he admitted to having been lost in Mont Tremblant Park. More than fifty years had to pass before he would let his pride waver. Progress, I suppose, but I still haven't heard about the walleye he stole from me, or about a thousand other things that I still prefer not to bring up. It's too late to start settling such large scores, but there may still be time to discover the human being hidden behind the fearful personality, behind the seemingly unemotional man. It's true that life didn't make it easy for him. A large family, blue-collar job, diabetes, uneducated well into his thirties—such things don't lead a person to happiness, or to culture or self-respect. Or any sort of delicacy of feeling. He hasn't a single personal memory that could be the subject of an impassioned conversation. He dislikes Arabs, Blacks and Jews. Anyone, in fact, who isn't exactly like himself. He's not really a racist, but he doesn't like being around Blacks; however, he's outraged by the Holocaust, and by what's happening between the Israelis and the Palestinians. He firmly believes that Americans are racists.

So, when we see my mother suffering from his old age, we worry about how much time she has left, and how much of it he may be depriving her of. In short, we worry that my father's illness is killing my mother. What a disturbing paradox, that a dying man can assassinate his perfectly healthy wife.

Mireille the Homeopath tells my mother that my father must be made to understand that exaggerating his illness will only make it worse. He's not stupid. Maybe there's some kind of therapy... What doesn't he understand? Life, his new life as a person who's dying? Mireille, would you accept the fact of your own death, sitting like this at a table groaning with cheeses and Christmas cake and bottles of wine, none of which you are allowed to touch? But I don't ask you the question. My mother is looking at me, knowing how much I would like to say something cruel, and nothing makes her sadder than to see her children, whom she loves equally, not loving each other the same way.

"Some wine, Mother?"

She perks up (amazing how she can shift from distress to obvious pleasure in a matter of seconds) and holds out her glass to let me pour her a finger of red. She looks up at me, pleadingly, it seems to me, though I'm not sure what she wants me to do. Probably not get into a discussion that she fears would end in discord. I think about the man who had to work so hard to lie down on his bed and let his eyes make their slow and painful voyage from the piano to the organ and the stereo. My father the deposed dictator, asking for a glass of wine, like Pinochet begging for mercy because he is old and senile. And so I speak up, wanting all the parallel conversations around me to stop, but of course they'll never stop in this family, and so I find myself speaking mostly to myself.

"Let's be serious here. Wine, cheese, bacon, fat, steak, never mind lobster and calf's liver—none of these things are good for Dad. And since emotions are also dangerous for him, it would be best if we deprived him of the pleasure—which is an emotion—of coming to our wedding. Walking isn't good for him, either. I know, he falls down regularly. He no longer likes to listen to music. He used to love the sound of his own voice and now he can no longer talk. We argue with him, tell him he can't do any of the things he likes, in the hope that it will prolong his life. We let him live while we await his death."

"You want to kill Mother."

The voice is both Medical and a bit Buddhist. My mother studiously nibbles a crust of cheese, like a mouse, oblivious to everything around her. She even picks up the crumbs from the table with two trembling fingers.

Two deaths have been announced. My father's death will free my mother, hers would kill him. A nice problem for a family.

I'm beginning to realize how hard it is to watch someone you've been living with for sixty years die, even if you don't love him. Just as it is to watch someone who's supposed to be dying go on living. I know how much my mother's life has shrunk since my father's began to end, neuron by neuron, and how, tired and defeated, she no doubt prays to God to give her back the husband she married. She has chosen to become the protector, the guardian, the nurse, but she also has to be the mistress of the house, the decision maker as well as the one who carries out the decisions. Did she choose that? No, probably not. Women of her generation have a sense of duty and long-suffering stoicism that benefit everyone around them, children, brothers, sisters, husbands. She has become both the father and the mother of the sick child that is her husband. If my mother is shrinking, it's probably because she is neither a man nor a woman, because she has assumed the responsibilities of both sexes and none of the pleasures. She doesn't actually live in her house, she functions. Although I understand these things, I say nothing. I keep my own counsel.

"Well, the neurologist told her that..."

The neurologist, as his title suggests, talks a lot about neurons but rarely about my father. He measures electric impulses, notes which ones are malfunctioning, describes deficiencies, forecasts storms in my father's brain and the destruction they will leave in their wakes. Neurons feel neither happiness nor pain. He, too, thinks that all strong emotions must be avoided—for electrical reasons, if I understand his explanations correctly. A too-strong emotional charge would overload the circuitry, possibly causing a power outage. At this he gave a small smile of satisfaction, apparently pleased with his own reductive joke. I asked about happiness. He replied that in such cases—that is, in the world of electricity—happiness and pain belong to the same family, demolishing in a few words everything previous generations have taught us when they said that happy people live better and longer lives than unhappy people. Science has progressed backwards. My father is an electrical panel.

My mother has turned the family room into a kind of pantheon to her successes and happiness, which means to her family and her children. We are seated in a kind of shrine, surrounded by icons. Each of us is represented by at least one photograph. We are actually visiting ourselves. My mother chose each photo after patiently going through the hundreds in her albums and boxes, which she dusts off regularly. Those of our children have places of honour. Then come my mother's favourite brothers, set beside her own mother and father. Then Richard at the piano. The biggest heartbreak of Mother's life, the schizophrenic child who could play Bach from memory, our whipping boy, who began to die the day he was born because of a stupid hospital error. If he were still alive, I'd be eleven months older than him. We went to the same school for two or three years, and everyone kept asking me why he was so backward, why he was so bad at skating or playing baseball, why he didn't always understand questions that were put to him, and if I couldn't duck the question I'd pronounce the fatal sentence, that my brother was a blue baby, he had a bad heart because he'd been deprived of oxygen at birth. I didn't want him to be my brother, just as in the supermarket, as I walked behind my father, who was dressed like a beggar, I wished he wasn't my father. I was ashamed of being my brother's brother and my father's son. I look over at Richard's photo, at the timid smile playing at the edges of his thin lips, and I am ashamed. One day my mother told me that Richard was aware of his failings and that that knowledge was the greatest of his sufferings. That was when shame and remorse overcame me. I should have been his hero, the one who protected him, tolerated him, accepted his difference with generosity. But to be that person, I would have had to know who I was and be satisfied with it. I hated being my father's son, hated being a member of his family, since the family was something he had created. When you feel small and insignificant, it's easy to seek refuge in spite, which is the pride of the weak.

"Yes, but what about Mother..." someone says.

"Yes, but Dad..."

I don't quite know why I'm so insistent tonight on my father's well-being and happiness. Normally our conversations about our parents' happiness centre on that of my mother, as though my father's happiness vanished forever with his diagnosis. Perhaps it's because my father hardly ever talks anymore, and when he does he seems to be giving in, almost as though he's trying to please us after so many years of arguing, grumbling and shouting. We know nothing of his desires, of his life—nothing. *We make it up.* My mother never hides anything from us. When she has indigestion, when she's constipated, when she cries or feels sad or angry. But the longer my father lives, the less we know him. We are condemned to speculate about a human being, which is a dangerous exercise.

"You should go over and talk to your brother. He looks sad. He seems to be somewhere else."

I find him hiding in the kitchen.

"Everything all right?" I ask, steering him into a corner.

"Yes, I've never been better in my life." He hesitates. "I'm having an affair, I'm crazy in love for the first time in my life. But I don't know what it is, with Mother I feel shy, as though she knows I've been cheating on my wife."

We've always known that we can keep no secrets from our mother.

"Have a glass of wine and relax, Claude. That wasn't what she thought. She thinks you're unhappy." But you'll let her in on your secret soon enough, because lacking something—I don't know what it is, maybe Dad—we vent ourselves on Mother, confide in her about our worst secrets, our most embarrassing weaknesses, we clamour for her help and understanding, her solicitude, her money, whatever we can get. Maybe that's why she's shrinking. With our wives and their lovers and our children and mistresses, it's like we're dumping fifty lives on her.

On the walls of the family shrine everyone has his or her *ex-voto,* except my father. In the great hall we are all heroes, except him. When I asked my mother why there was no photograph of Dad on the wall, she didn't hear me.

■   ■   ■

"NOW CAN WE OPEN OUR PRESENTS?" ¶
IT'S THE TRAGEDIENNE'S SON, THE ONE WHO
EXASPERATES HIS MOTHER BECAUSE HE IS NOT
doing well in school but amazes me with his gift for repar-
tee and his sense of responsibility. When I ask him about
his grades he pulls the universal adolescent face, which is a
way of transforming embarrassment into a refusal to show
any emotion at all. You'd think he was seeing the same
doctor as my father. His name is William, in honour of
Shakespeare. He's standing in the doorway and looking at
us with a sardonic, almost spiteful smirk, as though we're
all a bunch of degenerates.

He has a point. It'll soon be eleven o'clock and children believe there is more to life than eating, talking and
drinking.

Freed from the difficult task of organizing the lives
they've been trying to resolve, those attending the informal
family meeting at the far end of the table all shout joyfully:
Yes! The presents! Come here, children! Come sit by me,

my mother murmurs, but no one hears her. She smiles and places herself in the beatific circle of mothers who live only for their children's happiness. To whom was she speaking? As has been the custom in recent years, William takes his place in front of the enormous pile of presents and begins to distribute them. He produces a red Santa Claus toque and places it proudly on his head. Ho ho ho, he says, choosing a wrapped gift at random and reading the card on it.

"Grandpa..."

He looks around the room. Grandpa's asleep, someone says. We'll give it to him tomorrow, someone else adds. I don't think he's sleeping.

HE'S STARING UP at the ceiling. We can both hear the bursts of laughter and cries of happiness coming from the family room. He's a thousand miles from the Christmas tree, listening in on pleasures he can have no part of.

"I have a gift for you."

"Yeah?"

"Do you want me to open it?"

"No!... Give..."

It's an order. He says nothing more, but I understand. I should have expected his response, which more or less says he is still capable of untying ribbons and tearing off wrapping paper, of opening a gift and finding out for himself what someone has given him. I hand him the present. It looks like a book. He rests it on his chest and inspects a different part of the ceiling. He hands the gift back to me.

"I... don't... hmmm... my... glass... es."

I show him the book.

There's really nothing you can give a dying man that will mean much to him, except perhaps opiates or a good death. The former you can only get illegally, and a good death is hard to arrange. You might be able to find him a friend, but a friend isn't something you can pick up at the drugstore. This is a book, a beautiful one, about ancient Egypt, one of his great interests. It's the gift of someone who thinks he's still alive, a kind of acknowledgement of the militant autodidacticism of his past. A nice homage to this man with no formal education but who spent hours telling us about Ramses and Tutankhamen and the secrets of the pyramids and the riddle of the Sphinx. He opens the book, mutters something and closes it again.

"Too small..."

He seems so disappointed, so sad. And I don't know what he's trying to say.

"The... letters... too... small..."

"Mother says you need new glasses."

"No... too... ex... pensive."

He was never one to look after his body, as they used to say. He never played sports, always ate like a horse, and every night since 1954 he's fallen asleep in front of the television. As a kid I thought he was immortal because he only seemed to be bothered by other people's illnesses. Neighbours, parents. He didn't seem to believe in sickness, which probably explains why he never showed much concern about our infections or boils or childhood diseases. I never saw him being sick or even pretending to be. One of my sisters almost died because no one called the doctor when she had a simple ear infection. She'd been screaming with pain for a week. Finally my mother quietly rebelled and picked up the phone. Pus from the infection had almost reached her brain. The doctor practically had a fit. A cold here and there, all right, but not attending to a serious infection that could leave her deaf was as inconceivable to him as snow in summer. If my father was ever sick himself, he kept it from the rest of us. He must have been sick sometime, of course, but if so, no one knew about it. He would never be publicly sick, of that I'm sure. He was the kind of man who would never allow such weakness. That was the way things were. People around him were his principal subjects for conversation. He was the only one of us who never spoke about being sick.

"Grandpa!" Santa calls from the family room.

"No...more...presents...No...need..."

Which is what we ourselves have been thinking, more or less privately, for two Christmases now, each of us wondering what we could give him that wouldn't cause him pain. Some of us fell back on clothing, which he liked and accepted with big, toothless grins, the toothlessness not seeming to bother him much, as though having no teeth were the most normal thing in the world. But we noticed that he almost never wore any of the new clothes, and that my mother has stopped urging him to try them on. He seems content enough to await death with one pair of pants and one shirt, no need for more than one of each item of clothing.

William, who is also called Sam, our Santa Claus for the evening, comes into the living-room-turned-bedroom.

"Too... loud... they're... talking... too... loud."

A checked shirt, made from soft, smooth cotton. It was both muted and quite remarkable at the same time, like the clothes he used to wear when I hung back from him for fear of being noticed. Let me explain. In his Bermuda shorts and sandals he stood out in the supermarket aisles, no question, but the colours he preferred were always beige, or light brown, or soft reds, and these were much more of a whole, more muted, as I said, than the bright red ties and yellow shirts sported by the other, normal parents, or the checked pants that came along a few years later. It wasn't until I began hanging around with famous painters and other artistic types that I understood that my father didn't dress the way he did to attract attention to himself—if he had, he would have worn garish colours or the latest avant-garde styles. He simply dressed to be comfortable. As I write these words I wonder if he knew that people looked at him and his outfits with such distaste. Probably not, or he would have been mortified. I also wonder what form his pride took? That of a society man who simply wanted to stand out among equals, or the other kind, an individual who craved the freedom to be unique? Or yet another kind, a megalomaniac who wished to dominate, and whose actions required no excuse or even explanation? I think his is the perfect example of the pride of a man of his generation. I am what I am. Period.

Three Christmases ago he would have put this shirt on, its design and colours so perfectly matching his taste.

"Don't you want to try it on? It's the kind you always liked to wear when we went camping."

I mention camping because it's one of the few subjects that still interests him and sometimes gets him to brighten up, maybe say a few complete sentences. Mushrooms, travelling or rocks might also squeeze a few words from him when things are quiet, away from the relentless clamour of our family get-togethers. And since we're alone in his room with the background noise not much of an obstacle to conversation, I take the chance. He doesn't deign to respond, merely turns away and mutters to himself.

As I hold out the shirt to him I realize I've never seen him kiss my mother. Ten children, and not a kiss, not even on their anniversary. Dad, when you were making babies, my brothers and sisters, did you kiss Mother?

"Dad, the shirt is a present from... it's the kind of shirt you've always liked."

"Three... shirts... have... three... Enough."

If I were speaking to a child I would tell him to stop sulking, he's not a baby any more and he's making everyone feel uncomfortable.

"Stop sulking, Dad, you're not a child, after all."

He doesn't say anything. He looks off into space, or maybe at the piano. I don't give in to him. "Dad," I say. He mumbles something. Sam and I are dismissed.

■　　■　　　■

NOW IT'S MOSTLY THE CHILDREN WHO
ARE GETTING THEIR PRESENTS. OUR YOUTH-
FUL SANTA HAS FIGURED OUT THAT IT'S BETTER
not to pick gifts at random and run the risk of frustrating
the younger ones. Around the table, which is cluttered with
desserts, half-empty bottles of wine, wilted salads that no
one is eating, to the great annoyance of Lise the salad
expert, we are still talking about my father, even though
he's not here. Life may have totally deprived him of power,
but he's still here, dominating us as an ancient oak domi-
nates a landscape. The children are talking about a ghost
that haunts the house.

Buddhist or Medical, we all want the same thing. We
want to think that our parents are facing their deaths comfortably and peacefully. A simple enough desire, you'd
think, one capable of inciting a groundswell of support, as
the progressives would say, of uniting us at least as much
as it divides us. William is getting impatient. We're not
joining in the Christmas spirit. One of the sisters makes an

effort, tearing herself away from the conversation and making oohing and aahing sounds over an ugly doll.

The Medicals are addicted to crisp, cutting-edge science. They have their detailed reports, their lab tests, their cookbooks specifically designed for people with weak hearts and rigid Parkinson's, their neurologists, whose Mercedes-Benzes proudly proclaim their medical prowess. The Buddhists, of whom I am one (but only in this case), are not impressed with science, though they have nothing with which to match it from some other, equally solid and seated body of knowledge. We search the Net desperately, but come up empty-handed. We have no argument to make except that of the heart, or perhaps that of sentiment. Neither our affection nor our compassion makes us more human or more generous. We ask ourselves if the happiness of one parent is not the happiness of both. We quite simply refuse to believe that the beginning of death is the end of life. The Medicals, who have just as much heart as the Buddhists, oppose our position with a thousand little tangible tragedies, each of which is perceived as a tragedy for our mother. They are not afraid of choosing between dead and living futures. At the same time, they do not hesitate to impose life on those who are already well on their way to death.

The Medicals have opted for our mother. They've decided to save her life because of our two parents, she is the furthest from death. Our father must therefore die politely and quietly, so as not to cause our mother further pain.

Yes, I understand my mother's anguish, when she sees her husband, headstrong and arrogant as an adolescent who has just smoked a joint, leave the house to go for a walk, step onto an icy sidewalk and fall flat on his back after two seconds. Watching in desperation from the window, she sees the various parts of his anatomy trying to re-form themselves into a body. She sees that body lying on the icy sidewalk, not moving. That's what she sees from the window. I'm not making this up. She is the one who told me about it. She couldn't get him up by herself, so she rubbed his back, keeping him warm, encouraging him. She had to wait for someone to come along, or ring a neighbour's doorbell, in order to get this shell of her former husband back on his feet. I also understand her weariness, her fed-upness, when she saw him knocking himself out, shouting, getting more and more discouraged when he could no longer decipher bank statements or bills that made less and less sense to him, but which he nevertheless insisted on trying to take care of. For my birthday this past summer he sent me a cheque for twenty-five dollars, which I didn't get around to cashing. He had written down all of his expenses, all the electricity bills, the gas bills, the telephone and cable bills, and when he added everything up there was an extra twenty-five dollars in his account. He recalculated, reverified, went over everything again a dozen times, and ended up pounding his forehead with his fists. The next morning, my mother quietly went to the bank and withdrew twenty-five dollars from his account. They later agreed that banks were becoming more and more dismissive of their clients' needs.

What goes through his mind when he's told that washing dishes is too dangerous for him?

My mother smiles every time someone opens a gift and lets out a cry of joy. Calmly, I try to explain to her that she must give up her struggle to keep Dad alive as long as possible, but she keeps looking away, trying to see the gifts that are evoking such happiness. Actually, I don't say it in so many words. I don't actually say he's going to die anyway so we might as well let him die in peace, which is a ridiculous phrase, a falsely charitable cliché. I don't talk about death, I don't even use the word. I talk about pleasure. Westerners hardly ever speak of death, even when they're standing in the middle of a cemetery, and even less when it's the death of a close relative. I mention bacon and cheese, sausages and calf's liver. Surely once in a while it wouldn't hurt him. Another present is opened and she smiles automatically. The child shrieks with joy. All the wine bottles are empty. I get up, go into the kitchen for another bottle, and see my father standing in the doorway with exactly the same ecstatic smile on his face as is on the face of the ten-year-old who received the electronic robot he's been begging for for months. He has put the checked shirt on over the thick green sweater he was wearing. He's proud of himself. Beaming. Delighted with his little triumph and with the surprise he is going to give us.

"Dad, why are you out of bed? You should go back and lie down."

"Dad, why did you put your shirt on over that sweater? It looks terrible. It would go better with your jacket..."

"Come and sit down, Dad. You look tired."

Another child cries out. Heads turn towards the sound. My father goes back into his room. In the kitchen, I try to decide between the bottle of wine and my father, who I know is disappointed. I read a label, but it tells me nothing. I'm thirsty. I'm pretty sure my father is crying. I'm sixty years old, and I'm afraid to see my father cry. He walks silently towards his bed. Did Duplessis ever cry, or Stalin? I won't go into his room, even though I know I should. I don't want to see this man cry, this man I do not love and whose fall from grace is so upsetting to me.

I pour myself a large glass of wine. Lise, one of the Medicals, says jokingly that I must want to die, too, like Dad, who won't listen to reason. I drink too much, smoke too much, indulge myself with pork and foie gras and all the excesses of the palate, as well as of the night.

"At least I'll have a good death," I say. "I'll die happy."

"Asshole."

MY FATHER'S DEATH IS THE IDEAL MATH-
EMATICAL SOLUTION TO THE EQUATION WE
ARE SO GENEROUSLY AND AWKWARDLY TRYING
to solve. It would balance out the fundamental inequality
governing the relationships around the table. He is the
unknown factor that complicates all our algebraic calcula-
tions. How do we restore the equitable relationship
between my father, who is expanding, and my mother, who
is shrinking as she lives my father's death? How can we
ensure they both live equally happily? Can we invent a sort
of game in which no one loses? Our father dies, we cry for a
while—not for long, though, because we've all been expecting his death, even hoping for it, invoking it, albeit timidly,
in some far-off future. Then we move on to the next equation. Our mother. The Medicals can devote themselves to
her long survival, and the Buddhists can lead her towards a
joyful end. When there is only one variable in the equation,
two apparently contradictory approaches are more easily
reconciled.

And so the conclusion is reached. It's both simple and obvious. For everyone's good, including his own, my father must die.

I don't know if I'm drifting, rudderless, or if I've had too much to drink, or whether I really want my father to die. I can't stand to see him cry, this man who is known to me and is my father. A father humiliated by his illness, crying, is a man stripped of his essential being, no longer a father, simply a man like any other. And, worse, a naked man. Imagine a father, naked and crying. But I would prefer that to what he makes me feel now—anger, rejection, which is to say hatred. But that's no reason to kill him. I'm splashing around in the wine of my own contradictions.

As a child I prayed to see him cry, to see him brought low, bent in humiliation as I had been bent under his orders and condemnations, not to mention blows and insults. I would have given anything for him to be normal, like I was, proud or ashamed didn't matter, but just to show some emotion. If he was proud of me and my success at school, or in the theatre, which fed his own pride, he never said a word to me about it. It's my mother who tells me now how proudly and approvingly he spoke of me, how he tried to stammer it out to me before his neurons stopped communicating and brutally extinguished his retroactive congratulations. I was his son, of course I would be successful. It was as though long before they discovered DNA and cracked the genome code he'd already worked out his own theory of genetic inheritance, a theory that applied only to success, it seemed, because when my brother was sick he always referred to him, when speaking to my mother, as "your son," and never came to a play of mine that the critics panned.

Why did I bring up Stalin? Because I was living under the dull, daily threat of dictatorship at the same time that Stalin was appearing on television. They had the same smile, my father and "the little father of the Soviet nation." A snowy, black-and-white image, before televisions could deliver a true black: Stalin stood a head taller than all the other henchmen lined up looking martial and severe in their black homburgs. Stalin smiling under his thick moustache. A warm, engaging, confident smile. Looking out over Red Square with its rows of symmetrical regiments pouring through as though from an assembly line. The little father's tin soldiers, all walking with the same mechanical, chronometric precision. Stalin making a kind of salute by lightly lifting a hand that could just as easily have crushed a skull. To me it looked as though he were patting the head of every child in the world. I can't remember my father ever patting my head, or holding my hand, or putting a friendly hand on my shoulder. When the troops had filed past, Stalin turned and went back into his apartment in the Kremlin with his respectful model family. His children waited for a tiny, vague signal that told them it was time to laugh, or play, or run. The same was true for us at the dinner table, or when my father came into a room and interrupted one of our games. All activity stopped as we waited for him to send us to our rooms, or to go about in silence, which meant we could get back to what we were doing.

One of the Medicals asks me where Dad is. I tell him, a bit sharply, I suppose, but his curiosity exasperates me. It's merely a kind of clinical interest. Isabelle touches my arm, letting me know that I've overstepped the bounds of civility.

I'm thirsty. I reach for a bottle. Bernard cries out when he sees my arm stretch uncertainly towards his precious vintage wine, and he swears when I tip the bottle over. I laugh sheepishly, as though to excuse myself without admitting that I've done anything wrong. I feel like my father. Slight loss of control, no loss of pride.

"You're behaving like Dad when he does something stupid."

Like Dad? That's the only comparison I've never been able to stand. As I once explained to Mother, my first wife left me because, she said, I was too much like my father. It was partly true, but it was hard for my mother to hear, unfair of me to place such a heavy burden on her shoulders. To tell a wife that your life is ruined because you're too much like her husband. How stupid could I have been? She said, "You're exaggerating," and then all I heard was the empty buzz of the phone line. She'd hung up on me.

"Yes," I say. "Like Dad, Bernard, I'm overdoing it as usual..."

I indulge myself a bit. I like yanking Bernard's chain once in a while, making him face up to the stupendous absurdity of this life he is so awkwardly attempting to transcribe into equations. I'm old, Bernard, and part of being old is overdoing a few things, just as it is part of being young. Too much ice cream when you're a child, too much wine sixty years later. What should we do, forbid children to eat ice cream and doting old men to drink wine? Bernard blusters. Lise takes his side, blustering along with him. As far as they're concerned I'm being irresponsible. If I want to waste my life it's my business, but it's too bad for poor Isabelle, who in a few years will find herself wiping wine and grease and gravy off my chin. They don't say that, exactly, but it's understood. My mother refuses to be drawn into the discussion.

"What do you think of the election campaign?" she asks.

IN 1956, my father was selling cars. We hadn't climbed a single rung up the social ladder, but we were no longer drinking powdered milk. We had roast beef on Sundays, and my father wore a suit and tie to work every weekday. On Saturdays, however, when he did the shopping, he dressed like a slob. People don't really change. The living-room furniture was new. It was more comfortable than the old furniture, but we weren't allowed to sit on it except when we had company. On the walls were reproductions of great works of art I'd never seen before but that matched the colour of the fabric on the sofa and the wall-to-wall carpet. We had a television.

Except on Saturdays, when he dragged his noisy sandals down the supermarket aisles, we were a respectable family. I went to college, my mother wore pretty hats on Sunday, the flowers and shrubs my father had planted around the house were the envy of all the neighbours, who contented themselves with keeping their lawns green and nicely trimmed. He knew all that, knew he was envied, that he was accumulating points as if he were in a game, and he didn't bother trying to hide it. He revelled in his victories and advances, the apple tree that burst into generous bloom every spring, the client who couldn't afford a car but bought one anyway. He would call our anglophone neighbour over to show him how well his fertilizer was working. The neighbour, a timid man but an environmentalist before it became fashionable, would agree. We all bore witness to his successes, although we didn't really understand them. He triumphed. At the time I was getting 100 per cent in all my subjects at school; my mother crowed ecstatically but my father never said a word. I was his son, how could I come anywhere but first in class? My only merit, it seemed, was in being his son.

"ANYWAY, YOU'VE always looked down your nose at Dad and the family. The minute you became known as an actor... So we can do without your lectures, thank you very much..."

"I'm not lecturing, Bernard, I'm telling you how I feel."

Isabelle presses my arm again. In these circumstances she is smarter and more sensitive than I am. I'm a bit like an American. I charge into the fray and worry about the damage later. Isabelle is more African—she hears only what she needs to hear. In contemplating a lake, she knows that the pebble disturbs only the surface of the water, not the lake itself. It sinks without trace into the bottom mud, which is the lake's memory. And she's right. I should be more like Mother, who asks again what we all think of the election campaign, and questions me about my last trip to France, casting a worried look in Bernard's direction, knowing that if there is a silence Bernard will fill it with more talk about our father. Be more like Mother. Beat a dignified retreat. I stand up. Another present is announced. Another baby cries.

HE'S LYING half-naked on the quilt, having taken off the shirt and his undershirt, unbuttoned his trousers and pulled them down around his knees. He's breathing heavily. When he sees me come in, he turns his head into his pillow. There's nothing sadder or more disgusting than an old man lying like an abandoned doll on a bed, all his secret diminishments exposed. Or more pitiful. I don't know how the jovial Haitian woman who comes in once a week to give him his bath can stand it. Much less how she can wash twenty people like him every week.

I should undress him and get him into bed so that he'll be more comfortable. That's what the filial piety I do not feel would have me do. I have no intention of doing any such thing. I should at least cover him, maybe take off his shoes. I should go through the motions, not for him or the others, but for myself. So that I don't have to look at his flaccid body, splayed out so hideously on the bed. And what about him? How does even a passive racist like him feel about having those plump black hands washing and rinsing him, squeezing his flesh, running over his body? How does he meet her foreigner's gaze? What does he think as she washes his ears? How does he hide his sex? Is he completely naked in the bathtub? I can't even bring myself to imagine it. The bit of nudity I might discern in the shadows not only disturbs me, the whole thing is indecent. His jacket has been tossed onto a chair. I pick it up with the tips of my fingers and cover him with it, careful not to touch his naked body.

He might go to sleep.

In the family room the children are comparing their presents and the adults have fallen into my mother's trap. They're discussing the electoral campaign. My mother isn't really following the conversation, but she knows that when we talk about politics we are more likely to argue only about little things. She asks me what my father is doing. I say he's sleeping. She produces a smile meant to say, No wonder, he's eaten so much and drunk so much. She feels better knowing that he's asleep. It distances him.

"What about you, what do you think about the elections?"

"Mother, you know I'm not interested in politics."

"But you're an artist, you should be interested in politics. Many artists have spoken up..."

Yes, I know, Mother. But not me. I have nothing to say because I believe in so few things. She lowers her head to hide her disappointment. She goes up and down the street distributing pamphlets for the Parti Québécois, she never misses a chance to demonstrate against the war in Iraq or some other injustice. To make her feel better, I eat some of the orange mousse.

■   ■   ■

VENISE-EN-QUÉBEC IS A VILLAGE ON MISSISQUOI BAY FILLED WITH VACATIONERS WHO CAN'T AFFORD TO GO ANYWHERE ELSE. From here you can see across to the United States and imagine how rich everyone is over there. I'm thirteen, but I know that Venice is a city in Italy with a lot of canals, governed by doges wearing funny cone-shaped hats. In Grolier's Encyclopedia there is a photograph of the Piazza San Marco, showing the cathedral and pigeons swooping over the heads of visitors. I remember thinking about all the pigeon shit that must have been landing on all those well-dressed visitors. My parents are becoming increasingly worried about me, an adolescent who thinks about bombarding pigeons. But that's only a passing thought; in fact, I also think about cathedrals and history and the concept of a republic. Which is odd for a kid my age. I detect in my parents a mixture of pride in my academic achievements and dread, especially from my mother, when at supper my father says something I don't agree with. I think I said that Venice enjoyed a democracy that was far superior to that of Quebec.

I'm thirteen. This would be 1956. I'm the only kid in our neighbourhood who goes to college.

I'm not sure why my father invites me to go eel fishing with him. It's election day. He's already been to vote for Duplessis, because Duplessis is going to win and is not an intellectual, like Lapalme, who likes France and reads books. Duplessis is for Quebec. I'm a compulsive and opinionated reader myself. I may not understand everything I read, but I read only books from France. Plays, mostly: all of Molière, Racine, Corneille, but I have also discovered Ionesco and such poets as Prévert, Aragon and especially Éluard. I'm definitely not in Duplessis's and my father's camp. It's the only political statement I'll ever make in my life.

Lake Champlain is stormy, with a grey sky that promises rain. That doesn't bother my father, who always defies the elements, as the cliché has it. Quebec's Venice doesn't exactly live up to its name. Shacks—which their owners call cottages—covered with asbestos shingles, a few snack bars, tiny houses scattered in the sparse trees like splashes of red and green paint, popular music blaring out from everywhere—in short, a whirlwind of sound and colour and shapes, an ugly, deafening chaos. I think of the Venice in the encyclopedia. My father thinks it's idiotic of me to be surprised by the lack of similarity between Venise-en-Québec and Venice of Italy. He tells me not to talk so much, I'm scaring the fish.

I've never seen an eel, except in photographs in the encyclopedia. Before we left, my mother said defiantly that there was no way she was going to prepare eels. In our house, my father fishes and my mother cleans the fish and cooks them, obviously, except for trout when we're on a camping trip. Whether it's bullheads, with their skins as tough as shoe leather, or perch, which have razor-sharp dorsal fins, or walleyes, with spines sticking up from their backs, my mother wrestles with them while my father reads the newspaper, and later complains when he gets a bone stuck in his teeth.

Suddenly my line tightens, which is always the beginning of terror for me. This terror apparently delights my father. I remember the stolen walleye. What my father doesn't understand is that it's not the fish I'm afraid of, it's the bawling out, the lecture I get if I don't set the hook properly and the fish gets away after taking the bait. The ultimate humiliation. He looks at me, smiling like Stalin, as debonair as Duplessis, and begins discussing my line test, or the reel, which I am awkwardly rewinding. His laugh is that of someone tormenting a kitten with a ball of wool—not a warm laugh, but the laugh of a cruel spectator. I feel as though he's expecting me to fail, as usual, so that he can show me how to improve, he can demonstrate, teach, dominate. I pull a small eel out of the water and leave it flapping on my line on the bottom of the boat. It twists around like the snake it is, banging against the boat's hull making what seem to me to be dreadful noises that will scare away all the other fish.

"Get it off your hook. You're going to frighten the fish."

He's not laughing now. I grab the slippery thing close to its head and the rest of it wraps itself around my arm. I pull it off with my other hand and it changes arms. I panic. My father sighs, grabs the eel by the tail, swings it in a wide circle and smashes its head against one of the boat's seats. Satisfied, he rips the hook out of its mouth with a single swift motion. Nothing to it, my boy. You'll get the hang of it when you're older. He doesn't exactly say that, but I can see it in his eyes, in the condescension with which he looks at me. I put my line back in the water without rebaiting the hook. Over the next hour he catches five or six eels, each time showing me how it's done. Later I think I should have said to him: "Dad, you know that oldest rock, and those pyramids, and your eels, they don't interest me in the slightest." But I didn't say that and I'm glad I didn't. He wouldn't have understood that the last thing I wanted was to become a man like him.

THERE SEEMS not to have been a consensus of opinion on the electoral campaign, so my mother has turned to cooking to restore peace, or at least to make the conversation more orderly, less erratic, something linear that she can follow. Smoked fish. She loves smoked salmon, although it can sometimes be too salty. Trout is drier but less expensive, mackerel has too strong a taste, herring is too rubbery. We listen, nodding from time to time without knowing why, and I ask her if she remembers the eels.

"Oh, your father loved eel."

She puts on her angelic smile, which is both subtle and radiant at the same time, her remembering smile, like the smile of a child looking at a Christmas tree that seems to be lit by magic. She brings up more of her memories. We know most of them. Her close-knit, cultivated family, her heroic father, her legendary grandfather, her cousins who did nothing but read the most erudite of books, the intelligent gardens in which roses were so cleverly arranged they practically grew in the shapes of words. Whenever my mother brings up her family, my father withdraws, sighs deeply, groans. When he can get a word in edgewise he says we all know everything there is to know about her family. It's almost as though he holds the fact that she has a family against her. His own family has no place in his memories, or in ours. It's not that he's ashamed of them, although that's how it seems. His silence about them is worse, as though they're not even worth being ashamed of.

Feigning shyness, my mother asks for a refill of wine, adding that she's had too much already.

"What about you?" I ask her. "Do you like eels?"

"Oh, yes, I love eels, but in those days they weren't smoked, as they are now. We pan-fried them in wine."

Mother, Mother, with your angelic smile, why are you lying to me?

WE STOP BY the side of the road to eat our sandwiches and drink our cocoa. My father leaves the key in the "on" position so he can listen to the election results on the radio.

They're late coming in. I fall asleep, bored by the announcer's blah-blah-blah when he has nothing to announce, and tired of the relentless sarcasm from my father about my expertise as an eel fisherman. The same smile on his lips as when he points out a fault or a mistake. The blue-and-white Chrysler is cruising the streets of Montreal when my father wakes me up and announces triumphantly that the little father of the Québécois people has been reelected. The moment has weight, significance, in the history of Quebec society. Now I imagine how many tens or hundreds of thousands of people were at that moment exulting in the success of the Member from Trois-Rivières, like a family exulting in the happiness of the father, which assures the future of the children. I couldn't care less about any of it. I decidedly did not have a sense of family.

But I notice my mother's look of resignation when he deposits his six slimy eels on the kitchen table, as twisted together as a Gorgon. What a horror they are. He hasn't even said hello to her, although she's been worried sick because of our late return. He certainly doesn't notice the disgust and fatigue in her eyes as she looks down on the writhing snakes with blood oozing out of their torn mouths and running across the white top of the formica table.

"Best to prepare them now while they're fresh," he says. "We'll eat them tomorrow."

And he plunks himself in front of the TV to hear the latest news of the elections. My mother tells me to leave my clothes outside my bedroom door because they stink of fish, even though I caught only one. She also says to take a shower or a bath, as though I need to be purified. From the family room, my father shouts out the results and orders a cup of tea. He's the one who stinks of fish. He loves having physical contact with any animal he kills. Most people, when they take a hook out of a fish's mouth, hold the fish in one hand, close to the head, or if it's still wriggling or struggling to get loose, as the eels were, they immobilize them on the bottom of the boat with one foot. Not my father. Even if the fish is already half-dead, he lays it out on his leg or holds it tightly against his chest, as though saying to it: I didn't just catch you, I *own* you, I totally control you, you are going to die in my arms. Why is it that some men are so fascinated by violence? Does it prove their own power, or the weakness of the other? What pleasure does a child get from pulling the legs off a frog or torturing a cat? Is it a way of taking one's place in a world in which one knows nothing about frogs, or cats? Or women, or children?

"DO YOU remember the eels, Mother?"

"Oh yes, your father loved them."

"And you?"

"Oh, yes. But I didn't like cleaning them."

"But you did it."

"It made your father happy. Luckily he showed me how to do it. He made it look so easy. And the eels were so good."

One of the Medicals looks over when I mention eels, which is how conversations develop with us. A word floats between the stacks of plates, cuts through three other conversations and falls into the ear of someone looking for something to talk about.

"No, he can't have eels. Too much fat on them. They're like salmon. Dad cannot eat eels. Sole, maybe, or mullet, but only if they're grilled or fried in cold-pressed, extra-virgin olive oil. And not oil from Greece, either, because you never know where it comes from. I was in Greece one time..."

Yes, one time, in Greece, when she was so paranoid about being ripped off that she grilled some poor old codger about olive oil for a couple of hours.

My mother's no longer listening. She replaces covers on dishes, moves her plate around, nods yes a few times. I try to interrupt the monologue on Greek cuisine, but we're deep in Santorini, where there are no eels but the blues are divine and the houses are as white in reality as they are on the postcards, and the fried squid, which Dad of course can't eat, is tender and crisp, like french-fried seafood. When this woman talks about food, you'd never guess she is also a wise, dependable banker. She becomes a frustrated old bat. If she'd been robbed blind in Greece none of us would have minded. A child gives a shout of joy. The adults burst out laughing.

Our teenage Santa is mooning about the room like a lost soul. The younger children have gone back to their games and the adults to their conversations. He feels peckish and circles the table. There's no dessert left, he doesn't like cheese, the salad is wilted. There's a glass of beer on the table. He isn't allowed to drink beer but has been drinking it for the past three months with a kind of perplexed pleasure. He takes a mouthful and the bitterness makes him look around for potato chips, which make the absorption of this initiatory liquid less disagreeable.

"Grandma, do you have any potato chips?"

My mother pretends not to hear him, but the Banker instantly looks up. She was in the middle of a paean to feta, not just any feta but a certain feta from Thessaloniki that has just the proper sponginess, still milky and at its best after being marinated for hours in extra-virgin olive oil from Kalamata. Perfect with lightly grilled whole-grain pita. Greek bread is too floury. You can't get real feta in this country, but if you ever do, Mother, hide it from Dad. It's much too fatty for him.

"You children," she says to Sam, "you never think before you speak. Potato chips! Potato chips are not allowed in this house. They're dangerous for your grandfather. They could kill him."

I say not a word. My mother smiles and looks away in embarrassment. William or Sam ignores the Banker, as though she were a bad chess player who'd just advanced a useless pawn. His reply is a carefully thought out, resolute attack. A knight move. No, he says, no, he doesn't want to kill his grandfather, but his grandfather loves potato chips, and he doesn't think the little pleasure he derives from a few potatoes and a bit of oil and salt will kill him. My mother looks at him and smiles. Grandpa is dying of old age, he continues, because he is very old. He corrects himself: because he's older than Grandma. She smiles again, marvelling, obviously, at the mystery of adolescence. For adults, there is no more incomprehensible period in their children's lives than adolescence.

Adolescents are simply older children to whom we grant certain adult liberties so we can avoid confrontations that would remind us of the fact that they are still children. I cannot, for example, imagine a teenager being fascinated by death, that death would be something he or she would dream about, obsess over. But we prematurely confer on them the status of adulthood in order to avoid having to accompany them through their anarchic discovery of life. At least until they do something unusually stupid. Unsure of our own relationship to the real world, we prefer to think that they know everything we do not, which relieves us of the duty of having to teach them anything, explain things to them or forbid them anything. Forbid—a horrible word that no modern parents can use with their children.

Stalin and my father were true parents. They had all the answers and understood that children must remain children for as long as possible. Submissive, obedient children ease into adolescence for a troubling time, and then slide into adulthood and become good citizens without being aware of it. That's how adolescence makes men.

This adolescent looks up and says, simply: "I'll be right back, Aunt Géraldine."

A few seconds later he's back with two bags of chips, one barbecue and the other natural.

"I'm Grandpa's potato-chip pusher," he says. "Whenever I come to see him I bring a few bags. He hides them under his bed."

The Banker blanches and appears to be close to having an apoplectic fit. My mother hides a smile. Sam seems pleased by the stir he is making.

"Take a few deep breaths, Aunt Géraldine."

He laughs brightly, as though suddenly liberated from a great weight. She seems to have been robbed of the power of speech, she who with a wave of her hand regularly transfers tens of millions of dollars from Montreal to Zurich to the Grand Caymans to Panama, and back again by e-mail to Luxembourg. She finally rallies her thoughts.

"You want to kill your grandfather!"

"No, I love him as much as you do, but I want him to be happy. Shit, you never understand anything. You're older than he is."

The Banker's brows furrow threateningly and my mother tells Sam that it doesn't matter, she knew about the chips because under the bed isn't a particularly clever place to hide them. Sam beams.

My sister explodes. "You, too, Mother!"

"Of course, my dear. I know everything that goes on here because I still do all the housework and shopping.

Every now and then, when he's sleeping, I dump half a bag of chips in the garbage. I leave him a few treasures, let him have his little secrets, God knows there won't be many more of them. And I'm glad that William lied to me in order to make his grandfather happy."

Disconcerted, the Banker goes on about having a sense of responsibility, which my mother also appears to lack. Sometimes you have to refrain from making someone happy no matter how hard it is. Why, just two days ago she herself was eating a gargantuan plate of sauerkraut at the Berlin, she couldn't finish half of it, you really should go there, Mother, and she thought of Dad, who so loves sausages and pig's knuckles and smoked pork, but not for an instant did she consider bringing the other half home for him. Sometimes you have to protect people from themselves. Santa hesitates, then asks what he should do when Grandpa asks him for potato chips. Say no, of course, replies the Banker. Bring the chips, I tell him. My mother suggests not saying no, but maybe forgetting to bring them a few times.

The choice he makes now between my mother, my sister and myself will determine the larger chapters of his life later on, the decisions he'll make and perhaps, when he's an old man, ask himself why he made them. So much depends on a few bags of chips smuggled to an old man who is taking too long to die. I was always being told what to do, and I constructed my life around defiance. I'm fully aware that wine makes me fuzzy-headed, turns me in on myself, but I'm fond of Sam, and I'm the only gauge I have of what his future will be like. I cannot imagine it being very different from my own. So I think of him as a Santa Claus who no longer hands out Christmas presents, a boy who has kept the toque even though he doesn't like hats. Three roads have opened before him, each proposed by an adult whom he respects. It's no small thing for him, this dilemma; he is tossing two dice, Happiness and Death. As adults we talk about death and pleasure with detachment, with a certain distancing, to use a theatrical term, which allows us the freedom to speak in terms of concepts rather than real suffering. Children don't have that luxury. They live in the concrete, they know only the here and now. Words do not have hidden meanings, they're as full and round and perfect as billiard balls. To them, words are like fragmentation bombs. They explode in our faces. Sam is discovering that love can kill and cruelty can be kindness, that life is not simply an endless quest for happiness; sometimes you have to live with pain and sorrow, and it may even be that we have a duty to keep people alive who are in agony or despair. Fine, then; he's not an idiot and he knows that potato chips won't kill his grandfather. The knowledge reassures him slightly, but not completely.

My mother stands up as we clear the table for the third time. In a voice she imagines to be resolute, she advises Santa to do what his instinct tells him to do—act according to his feelings. Poor kid. He doesn't want that kind of freedom in a world he doesn't understand, a world of old people and their happiness or their death. He prefers the

Banker's ban, or my own permissiveness. He feels comfortable with either. We represent, for now, the two poles of his life. No. Yes. My mother doesn't want him to take chips to his grandfather, but she sacrifices this principle, she thinks, to that of making the child happy. Her affection for him has drawn her astray; it makes her grant him the intelligence she thinks he already possesses. Choose, decide, change, evolve—this is the complex, dark rhythm of intelligence whose travelling companion is feeling. Sam sits in my father's chair to catch his breath, to give himself time to think, as though it's easier to come to a decision sitting down than standing. My mother goes on about the beauty of youth, its generosity, saying what every real mother says: You thought you were doing the right thing, and that's what counts.

But no, that's not true, William thinks. If doing the right thing means killing him, then he doesn't want to do the right thing. He doesn't say that, but that's the thought that's tormenting him. What will he retain of those three choices, the ones that determine the book of his life from now on? He's fourteen, or thirteen, I forget which, and his life is taking on a definite shape. Submission to facts and logic, or the senseless search for happiness, or a sort of self-indulgence that navigates between the two. Those are the unanswerable questions he will ask himself when he leaves here. I've been watching him, and I know that like my mother, he has shrunk. His shoulders have become stooped, he looks vaguely around at nothing in particular. He's on the cusp of old age. What's important is not the choices he'll make, but that he knows from now on that every gesture is weighted, and that he must think before he acts. A bag of chips has just launched him from childhood into an age in which games and innocence are not allowed, since they are just a nobler form of ignorance. I look at Isabelle, who's engaged in a passionate discussion with one of my sisters about fabrics. If she is the incarnation for me of lightness and cheerfulness as much as she is of determination and reflection, it's because she never, not for one instant, has been pushed further than her age, because she lived all the days of her childhood and was only subtly transmuted into the hours of adolescence, then, when the time was right, to the minutes of adulthood. The further we progress, the faster time passes.

My nephew gets up. As he passes behind my mother he bends and kisses her tightly curled hair so lightly she doesn't feel it. He smiles faintly. He walks like an adult towards either the gallows or freedom, straight as an arrow, his head thrown back as though to make it easier for the hangman to slip the noose around his neck, or perhaps to have a better view of the roads opening up before him. His shoulders become even straighter when he reaches the gang of kids playing loudly with their new toys, fighting over them, and he strides through the piles of wrapping paper, flattened boxes, decorative bows and scattered ribbons. The children are still children. They haven't yet understood that their grandfather is no longer the grandfather they have known all their lives. Only that he walks more slowly and doesn't talk so much.

Santa takes off his toque, which now seems a ridiculous thing to be wearing, and speaks in a low voice. Five or six of the younger children also lower their voices and begin methodically picking up papers and organizing toys, with the long faces of those who have been caught red-handed in an act of criminal thoughtlessness, which in the eyes of adults is the worst crime a child can commit. A bit of order and silence in this joyous chaos and continuous noise is what the new adult seems to have decreed. What did he say that put such a quick end to the celebrations? Grandpa is sick, probably, if he doesn't sleep he'll die, be quiet, stop shouting, and Grandma is tired, we have to tidy everything up. The children carry out his orders like a battalion of servants. A few parents notice, including Santa's mother, who says sharply: "It's Christmas. Children are allowed to enjoy themselves..."

Her son looks at her as though she is a war criminal.

"You want to kill your father?"

I pour myself more of the wine I've already had enough of. Santa's mother tells him to take a few deep breaths, her attempt at humour. He doesn't understand her lightness, her devil-may-care attitude. I stand up, a little shakily, under the anxious gaze of Isabelle, who, I sense, takes a motherly interest in my slow progress between the chairs and the children and the piles of paper. When I reach William I pick up the Santa Claus hat that he's dropped and put it on my head.

"Sam, would you like me to beat you at ping-pong?"

"All right, but after that I'll demolish you at chess."

DESPITE THE WINDING DOWN OF THE
YEARS I CAN STILL BEAT WILLIAM AT PING-
PONG, AND DESPITE THE YEARS HE STILL HAS
ahead of him, he always humiliates me at chess.

But this time the ping-pong game doesn't fit the pattern. I'm more interested in enjoying myself than in defeat-
ing my opponent. This is partly because I know I'm a better
player than he is. In other circumstances it would be called
having a superiority complex. I miss all my slams, which
normally are my specialty. Sam laughs mockingly and
tempts me with high lobs that look easy, and which I smash
one by one into the net. He plays methodically and defen-
sively, the way I play chess. I continue playing an attacking
game, slicing the ball or putting backspin on it or hitting it
as hard and, I hope, as decisively as possible. I put my faith
in aggressiveness and instinct, on my reflexes, as William
does when he plays chess. The chess master who is giving
him lessons says that when logic settles into his imagination he'll be a genius. I fall behind, Sam laughs more and
more. I miss another slam, an easy one. Sam stops laughing

even though he's never been a humble winner. He needs one more point to beat me once and for all. Ever since we began pummelling each other every Christmas over this wobbly table in this narrow basement, banging our heads on the water pipes that thread through the rafters, ever since Christmas has existed and Sam has been old enough to hold a racquet, he has been waiting for this moment. His first victory. He sets his racquet on the table.

"I don't want to play anymore," he says.

"You only need one more point to beat me."

"You're not playing seriously. It doesn't count. It's like you're letting me win."

"Come on, finish the game!"

I want him to have this first win. A Christmas present he'll always remember.

"Do you love Grandpa?"

Most of all I don't want to answer that question. "Come on, it's your serve."

"Tell me. Do you love Grandpa?"

"Do you?"

"Yes."

He says it without hesitation. His answer thunders across the table at me like an unreturnable slam. He's defying me now.

"Serve the ball!"

He serves me a soft, easy one, and I flick it back to his corner. Twenty-twenty. I win a point on my spinning serve. He misses his own. I've won.

"Okay, you win, but you haven't answered my question."

No, my boy, I haven't answered the question, because...
I offer him another chance to beat me. He declines. He has
chosen his field, his sport: truth, a curious game that rarely
produces winners. Still, I try to beat him at it.

"So, why do you love him?"

I'm hoping for a surprise attack. My opponent was
waiting for a backspin, but what I've sent is an overhand
topspin that hits the table and takes off like a rocket on a
downward curve. He returns with a strong, hard backhand
that catches me off balance.

"Because he listens to me and doesn't judge me."

Okay, his point. But now it's my turn. I'm not about to
let myself be beaten when the subject is my own father.

"Well, Sam, it's easy to listen when you can't talk."

"He can talk, you just don't understand him. And you
still haven't answered my question."

Two-love for him. An upset in the making. In any
match there's a point at which you can recover from a stra-
tegic error by stepping back and allowing yourself to lose
another point in order to improve your position on the
field, or you can stay on the attack, throwing caution and
restraint to the wind.

"No, I don't love him."

"I understand what you mean."

Now it's three-love Sam. Choosing his words carefully,
he explains to me that he doesn't love his mother, either. He
likes her well enough, but more as you would like someone

you knew well, someone with whom you had something in common, to whom you owed something or someone you could count on. He doesn't for a moment want me to think he's passing judgement on his mother, on her quality as a mother.

"I'd rather have parents who were older, who had no other life left than that of their children."

"Why, so you can be free to do whatever idiotic thing comes into your head?"

"No. Christ, you can be a jerk sometimes. How can I explain it? So that I don't have to be told that you can't make a living playing chess because chess players don't have time to learn things like grammar and trigonometry. Do you know who Bobby Fischer is? Well, do you think Bobby Fischer did his homework? No, he worked on his openings."

And I learn that my father knows how to play chess quite well. No, I'm not learning that, I am remembering how, when I was four or five years old, he plunked me down in front of a piece of wood with little tin soldiers on it and tried, without the slightest success, to teach me the patient yet cunning advance of the pawns, the sneaky strategy of the knights, and the overwhelming power of the queen. I didn't understand a thing, and he mated me in two moves, the classic trick of fathers who want to impress their children even as they're humiliating them. Since I'd already been humiliated a hundred times, I decided to loathe the game and take pleasure in disguise and imagination. By which I mean the puppet plays I put on for my brothers and sisters, and declaiming the poems of Rimbaud at school concerts to parents who were shocked to discover that their children were learning things as ridiculous as "A red, U black..." and what's this about a boat that has had too much to drink, and Ionesco, whom I understood not at all except that the dialogue in *The Bald Soprano* resembled the rare conversations I'd had with my father.

"Anyway, that's what I mean. When Grandpa was still talking, he asked me what I wanted to do with my life. I said, Bobby Fischer, and the next minute we were playing chess. I beat him easily, but he was happy that he'd at least put up a good fight. Can you imagine it? Your father, who has even more pride than I do, smiling after losing a game of chess? Since then we've become friends. With my mother it was hopeless. She sort of understood the pawns, but after that, nothing. I beat her in five moves, and you can take it from me, she wasn't happy about it. Grandma doesn't know the first thing about chess, not even who Bobby Fischer is. But she cuts out all the accounts of chess matches in the newspapers. I offered to teach her the basic rules, and Grandpa burst out laughing. He looked at me like I was one of his buddies and I would understand why he laughed. Before a tournament, I come here and explain my tactics and strategies to them. They drink tea and listen without understanding a word I say, but they never interrupt and then they ask me to phone them after each match to tell them how I did. Okay, maybe I'm wrong, but it seems to me that only old people know how to listen. Maybe it's because they don't have much of a life of their own that other people's lives interest them so much. All parents do, though, is talk."

"And that's all they do to make you love them, is listen?"

"No, they talk, too, but only to answer questions. And they don't answer them the same way. It's like they take more time than parents do, or teachers. They think about things. Maybe they have to go back over their whole lives before they reply, or like they have so many memories and experiences that they know it's not easy to give answers. I don't know where all these words are coming from, because I don't usually talk like this, but believe me, their answers give us our freedom."

Answers that don't say no, that invite reflection. I'm discovering parents, especially a father, I've never known.

It's time we went back upstairs and rejoined the tribe, at least for me. I've learned a bit about my nephew, which is enough for me. And Isabelle will be looking for me. My father is probably asleep, and that thought I find comforting.

"William, do you really not love your mother?"

"Yes. No. I love her the way anyone loves their mother. But at my age it's hard to love. No, I love her, but not like I love my grandparents. When I see them, I always feel like it's for the last time. Don't you think that makes it easier to love them? And Grandpa seems so happy when I'm around. That makes it easier to love him, for sure. Mom doesn't make it easy. And neither do I. I don't give her a lot of chances. Maybe if I thought Mom was going to die, I'd love her more."

"Or maybe you'd run."

"No, I wouldn't do that. I may not be a good son, but I don't hide from her."

■　　■　　■

FROM UPSTAIRS COMES A SOUND LIKE
ALL THE FURIES OF HELL HAVE BEEN LET
LOOSE. OOHS AND AAHS, BABBLED SHOUTS IN
which words are lost in intense discussion that dissolves
into bouts of nervous laughter from several other adolescents. I hear Penelope, Sam's sister, with her piercing
voice:

"Grandpa!"

"Couldn't... sleep... uhh!... too... noisy..."

He's back.

He's standing in the kitchen doorway, looking dazed,
naked from the waist up, the skin on his breasts and stomach sagging in pools of flab. He weaves a bit on his feet
and smiles beatifically. The adults have gone quiet. Silence
reigns, mixed with terror. It's the first time we've seen our
father as he really is. We only know his face and his symptoms, the diagnoses, the signs, we've never seen him looking so diminished, so naked, so ugly. We knew about his
wobbling, the slurred speech, the fact that he falls regularly,

belches, sleeps in his chair and drools in his soup. We've seen all that. We are familiar with his illness, but not with his ugliness, or his exposed feebleness. "You should get dressed," my mother says. She isn't worried about how he looks or what we are thinking. She knows all about how he smells, his folds and wrinkles, his flaking skin, the liver spots that make him look like a pale leopard, and the idiotic smile he makes when he's not quite sure what he's doing. She has borne ten children and sees him now as nothing more than the eleventh, who has to be told to put something on so he won't catch cold. That's all she's worried about at the moment, a draft of cold air, a sudden chill. But she's no longer of child-bearing age, an age of worrying about a draft that could get into a child's lungs, or even an age of having a husband who nibbles away at the last few happinesses of her life and who, like a baby, shrieks when the bottle isn't warm enough. It's his health she worries about. While we worry about our own terror. When I see him, I'm afraid of my own old age.

Sam is the only one who doesn't share our thinly veiled disgust. I see the Commander, who comes on stage at the end of *Don Juan*. Is he going to take me by the hand and lead me into the flames of hell? No, my father is not Death as he appears on stage, or on the screen—he is ridiculous death, a statue lacking lustre, ordinary death showing itself unselfconsciously on Christmas Eve. Sam and my mother move towards him at the same time, drawn by the same compassion, the thoughtless generosity of those who are never held back by pity or commiseration. Sam has taken off his pull-over. My mother takes my father's hand and leads him away. Someone tries to say something funny: "Are you trying to frighten us, like you did when we were little?" Yes, he says. Sam puts his sweater over my father's shoulders and my mother ties the sleeves around his neck to make a cape. On the television, which has been turned down, a priest is lifting the sacrament above his head. The camera pans across the crèche and slowly zooms in on the Baby Jesus. Cut to the priest lifting the chalice to his lips and drinking the blood of the child he has just displayed to us.

My mother and Sam help him sit in his chair at the head of the table, facing the TV, and he asks for the sound and more bread. The Agnus Dei fills the room and stops both adults and children in their tracks. My father taps his fingers on the table while waiting for his bread. For years before we moved into this house, he sold bread for a living. He's not proud of that time, especially since he was working for Weston Bakeries, but bread is the security of the poor, the staff of life. It fills the stomach cheaply. He was poor and so he became hooked on bread. At least that's what I think when I see him grab a crust that has fallen onto the tablecloth as though he has dug up a black truffle. He'll eat any kind of bread, no discriminating. The crustiest baguette, American white bread, the olive-and-sun-dried-tomato bread served in all the trendy restaurants, hard-as-a-rock organic bread that the Homeopath brings over, cheese bread, round loaves that we used to call bum bread, rye bread, ten-grain bread. He eats it dry or soft, stale or fresh, buttered, smothered with jam or cheese or melted pork fat, margarine or pâté de campagne. But now that he's sick, the chances are good that bread will kill him.

Sam has come back from the kitchen looking serious and thoughtful. My father is smiling. My mother is looking sad or resigned or exhausted, it's hard to tell at this stage. Santa has taken up his role as gift giver again, and my father gets a loaf of bread. Sam puts his hands on my father's shoulders and whispers in his ear.

"Eat, Grandpa," I think I hear him say. "Eat your present."

"Good...pres...ent...thank...you..."

And he stuffs bread into his mouth without looking up from his plate.

"Sam, I don't know why you want us to keep calling you Sam. You'll be a man, my nephew." He doesn't know Kipling, but if he'd been my son...

"William is too serious. Sam sounds more like me."

The diffuse family murmur resumes like a rumour passing through a village. My father eats, grunting with pleasure. Sam turns off the television.

At the far end of the table the Homeopath stamps her foot. She's not a bit happy. You'd think she was the one being pushed into an early grave by being force-fed bread and cheese. I watch her blanch when I pour some wine into my father's pewter cup. In desperation, she tries catching my mother's eye, but my mother has withdrawn into some secret place located somewhere on the tablecloth, at which she stares without looking up, gently nodding her head. She is out of service. She has too many children tonight. The queen of natural health stands up brusquely and wraps her seventies scarf around her shoulders. Eyes firm, back straight, step determined. I steel myself for intemperate declarations, moral lessons. I try closing my ears. Isabelle says this is going to go badly. How has she learned to read my own family so well? The Homeopath doesn't waste time chewing out Sam, who is the object of all her resentment, nor does she rebuke my mother. She goes straight for my father and takes his plate.

"That's enough! This is unacceptable! It's not good for you, you must understand that."

"No!" my father shouts as though someone were trying to hang him. With a hand that is suddenly strong and sure, he grabs the pewter cup. Both cup and wine sail out into the air.

"Dad!"

A spontaneous cry from the adults in the audience.

"My beautiful shawl!"

I'm not sorry to see it go; it was one of those old-fashioned shawls with bulging fringes, like sideburns. I almost laugh at her anger, at the way she spreads the shawl over the seat of her chair and starts shaking salt on it, impatiently, because the salt runs so slowly. "Christ!" she says, unscrewing the lid of the shaker and emptying it onto her precious accessory. And I learn a few more things. That the shawl came from Boston, where she bought it in a fit of amorous delirium when she and her American boyfriend were demonstrating against the draft, and that this seemingly reserved woman is capable of swearing and even of being carried away. I've always thought of her as an obligatory homeopath, incapable of anger and blushing and passion. Anyone can make a mistake. We make mistakes all the time.

Who, then, is she? The sour-tempered woman who lectures my father about slices of bread, or the one who's in tears over a souvenir of a vanished America, or maybe of smoking a joint in the nude on a beach in Cape Cod? The one who always says Excuse me before speaking, or the one who spits Christ! because her father stained her shawl with a glassful of forbidden wine?

I know the answer now; she is all those women, and I apologize to her for having always seen her as a caricature. Flat, no depth to her at all, not structured like the earth that is built up in layers so as always to be evolving and hiding its secret origins, and into which you have to dig, penetrate, if you want to understand it. In despair now that her shawl is soaked with wine, like all the other old things that are brought back to life, she gets up, goes over to my father and accuses him of having destroyed one of her most precious memories. All because of a love that no one could have guessed existed. An absurd love for what once was but which surely can no longer be. A beach. A fire, a joint for him, a glass of wine for her. A night. A shawl. My father smiles. He always smiles when he can't hear what's being said but senses it's about him. He who never smiled at anything we said now resorts to this dolphin's rictus as his ultimate defence. She lowers her head, withdraws from the fray, having realized that despite the brouhaha no one is interested in her shawl. She retreats to the kitchen, where she tries to soak a stain out of a part of her life. This is how memories, which are layers, get installed and never leave us. I will always remember her Boston, she will always remember our indifference to it. Who is right? No one.

The flying wine cup ended its trajectory in my mother's face, and her eyebrow is bleeding profusely—a real boxer's cut, not dangerous but a wound from which blood pours as from a faucet. While my sister dies a little over her ruined shawl, the rest of us bend over our mother. The Banker says we have to call 911, others respond that it's not that serious. My mother takes her napkin from her lap, pushes off the apprentice doctors and presses the napkin to her cut. My father puts his hand over hers.

"Press... press... hard..."

He keeps his hand on hers and repeats: Press, press. He is not smiling. He is concentrating. I hear a voice almost telling him to leave her alone, and from its tone comes the sense that he is too old to help his wife, too impotent and infirm, and that in any case it's his fault that she's bleeding. But he no longer hears the nasty comments. He may hear the words, but he can't possibly imagine that he is the object of some reproach. He never does anything wrong. He only tries to assume his responsibilities.

Now he puts his other hand on my mother's hand holding the napkin, which she removes from time to time to see if the blood is still flowing. Press, press, he says, and I don't know quite how but he manages to get up and stand behind her and press her forehead with both his hands.

"Band...aid...band...aid...Christ..."

A murmur spreads through the room, a murmur of shame keeping its voice down. We call to one another, our eyes darting everywhere. Band-aids, where are they, do you know? We thought of everything except band-aids. I can feel humiliation rising like vapour from the Banker, the Homeopath and the Geographer. Even though they have no feelings in common, they know that when it comes to their mother's and father's health they are part of the clan. They're the ones responsible. They look tentatively at one another, discussing what to do, but no one moves. Including me. I look at my father, still pressing my mother's forehead with his two hands, staunching the flow of blood.

I THINK IT WAS my Uncle Bertrand who used to own a cottage in Bois-des-Filion. An old tumbledown shack on a dirt road that led to a small patch of beach. On summer weekends, families would install themselves along the sand in the same way they lived in the city. Shoved up against one another like the houses they inhabited. My father couldn't stand the closeness of it. If he had to leave the city he wanted room, he wanted to be able to contemplate the river without being disturbed. He would leave early in the morning, when all the other shacks along the road were still reeking of bacon and eggs, the children still getting cleaned up and the parents yawning or belching up their beer from the night before, and he would secure our position at the far end of the beach, beside a thin, dead pine, all that remained of nature, but enough to symbolically separate his few square metres of sand from the Ideal Beach Dance Hall, which is what this particular stretch of beach area was called. He would mark off his territory, our territory, by tracing a large border in the sand with his heel, placing the cooler and two folding lounge chairs in the centre of it under a large beach umbrella, spreading out a few towels and then, satisfied with his arrangement, wait for the rest of us to arrive, led by our mother. He would wait standing up, scornfully eyeing the other families bunching up on top of one another, not daring to come near this scowling figure with the face of a cop or a bandit. Once Mother arrived and the children were gathered, he would take his book, sit in a chair and forget about us. If one of us seemed in danger of drowning, it was our mother who ran into the water to save us. If we fought with the kids next to us on the beach who had no notion of territoriality, it was my mother who settled the dispute. My father would indicate his displeasure, multiply his decrees, grunt a few times, but he would take no part in the life of the beach except to keep watch over our own square of sand.

One Sunday we were returning from Ideal Beach with Uncle Marcel, who sold used cars. There were five of us in the back seat of his blue Chevrolet with the Monarch fenders and the Chrysler steering wheel and the window cranks serving as door handles. Uncle Marcel made his living doing a little bit of this and that. When my father told me to open the window wider because it was too hot in the car, I obeyed like the good little soldier I was, without thinking or looking at what I was doing. I turned the window crank and the door opened; out I tumbled, onto the shoulder of the road and into the ditch. It was my mother who leapt out of the car and ran to save me. Blood was pouring out of my head like water from a hydrant. My father never lost control. He waited calmly in the car until my mother brought me back, then got into the back seat, held my head on his lap, pressed some sort of cloth to my wound and held it there with his two large hands for the thirty minutes it took us to get to the hospital. I was moaning, my brothers and sisters were crying, my mother was trembling. He never said a word the whole way, just sat there pressing on my head, squeezing it tight, blocking the flow of blood. He was in control of the situation. My mother said I was lucky. A fractured skull. Still my father said nothing, not even when I came home from hospital, my head wrapped in bandages but otherwise saved at last.

SAM, WHOM I no longer wish to call William, reappears, his eyebrows knitted and his forehead creased with the responsibility he has taken on. On the table he sets down the cotton batting and gauze and an assortment of bandages. He has brought in the entire contents of the bathroom cabinet. Two girls follow him in, each issuing advice that sounds more like orders. My father grunts. They freeze. My father points a finger at one of the band-aids, a thick, square one. Sam takes it and holds it up to my mother's eyebrow, which is still being pressed by her own and my father's hands. He says yes and leans over. They take their hands away. The cut bleeds a tiny bit, Sam puts the band-aid on it, and then nothing happens. My father, breathing heavily, bestows an incensed look on each of the rest of us in turn. Sam presses on the bandage until the bleeding stops. Like an impotent idiot I watch my father's anger becoming more and more visible. Isabelle quietly picks up a roll of adhesive tape and puts it in my hand. My father nods. For several seconds I am a child again, guilty, not understanding what it is I'm supposed to do. Sam beats me to it.

"Not...quick...e...nough."

And he says ha-ha, which is the only expression of mirth remaining to him, the written form of laughter that he reproduces verbally, since his malfunctioning neurons no longer allow him the joyful delirium of a disorderly outburst of sound that is not well relayed by this symbolic and simplistic onomatopoeia. It is a triumphant, proud ha-ha. The father expressing his condescending yet at the same time fond contempt for his children. Essentially it says: Without me they are nothing.

My mother's right eye has disappeared under a swath of gauze bandaging. She looks like a First World War victim, hastily treated in the Verdun trenches by a clumsy but well-intentioned medical recruit. My father is now beside himself with his ha-ha's. He points a finger at his curiously enwrapped wife and shouts, "Pho... to... pho... to..." The Geographer is not laughing. He doesn't say that the wound hasn't been disinfected, or that the bandage doesn't have to go over Mother's eye, and in any case this is not something about which we should be laughing, but that's what he's thinking. Instead, he acts like a Japanese tourist. His top-of-the-line digital Canon explodes with flashes of light a dozen times. He circles about, covering all the angles, even peremptorily asking the victim to turn her head a little to the right, where the light is better. My father relaxes, satisfied and perhaps even happy. The Homeopath is back talking about her Turkish delight. Most of the adults get up and tackle the pile of dirty dishes in the kitchen. Emma is asleep in the arms of my daughter, who is yawning herself. Her boyfriend is discussing GICs with the Banker. The other children are taking turns playing Donkey Kong, their bodies and brains totally involved in a furious tournament that has all the appearances of a desperate struggle for survival. If it weren't for my father's semi-naked body—which everyone seems to have forgotten about except my mother, who looks at him from time to time with her good eye and blinks at the incongruity of it—anyone looking in on the scene from the outside would think this was a boring, predictable gathering of a middle-class family.

"GRANDPA," William says, "I have a present for you. It's from me. You were asleep earlier, and I didn't have time to give it to you."

He smiles like a child who is proud of himself. He is holding one of those boxes made to contain a bottle of wine or alcohol. "He's not going to open it tonight," someone says, "he's had enough to drink as it is." Sam doesn't move. My father and I are also halted by this Medical injunction, which comes like a police order to cease and desist. It's a Minervois, Château Villerambert-Julien 2000, says Sam, recommended by all the Quebec guides and even by the Nicolas Web site, the biggest wine merchant in France.

My father looks at the bottle as though it were a Grecian amphora. His eyes glisten with happiness.

"Thank...you...my..."—a long pause—"...friends."

He called us "friends"!

ALTHOUGH MY FATHER WAS CATHOLIC, HE WOULD HAVE SKIPPED MASS TO GO TO A SALE. HE OBSERVED ALL THE RIDICULOUS RULES of Catholicism—fish on Fridays, three hours' fast before taking communion, crossing himself at the same time as the priest. But whenever he had to sit through a religious ceremony or a sermon, he went to sleep. With the first snowfall in December, however, his life was transformed. As Christmas approached the house filled with carols and my father was home more often than not, took more liberties with his work schedule, spent hours shopping for a Christmas tree, left the phone for my mother to answer and rarely returned calls, even to clients. He visited the curate to hand in his tithe and went to confession, another once-a-year ritual. He spent a great deal of time in the basement, getting out the boxes in which he'd stored the crèche and the Christmas ornaments, checking the lights, ringing the little bells to make sure they weren't cracked. He combed the stores and boutiques looking for the perfect gift, the clever surprise, the game that was all the rage, the present he would like to have received as a child. He invited all the family members he didn't like to dinner, and informed them coldly that he didn't need anything.

And then on Christmas Eve he imposed the purest torture on us. Not only were we forbidden to touch or, God forbid, shake the presents that were piled under the tree in the family room while Mother was downstairs wrapping the rest, we weren't even allowed into the room. We had to look in from the kitchen. We'd been used to this since the first time our bottoms were smacked, which invariably happened at the age of three, as though that were the point at which children's backsides became tough enough to withstand his assaults. The older children had to help put up the tree, silently, then arrange the lights, an exercise he seemed to have thought a lot about. Once a string of lights was in place he'd step back, study the tree, grunt, rearrange the bulbs according to colour, break off a small twig that worked against the desired effect. He moved methodically, with the air of a man obsessed with a mission. He would tolerate no interruptions, no comments or suggestions. We had to admire the great creator of the Christmas scene. On the other hand he would regularly turn to us, like an actor seeking the approval and applause of his audience. We would remain quiet, our silence guaranteeing our immunity. Once the lights were installed he would place the icicles on the tree, then the ornaments, the candy canes, the cloth Santa Clauses, a few tinkling bells that he'd saved for just before the final, crowning achievement, the star on the summit.

"You moved the red ball," he said, looking at me.

There were twenty-five red balls on the tree.

There was no point in my denying having moved it, even though any one of the three brothers looking down at the floor could have been the culprit. He knew it was me. I was the delinquent, the one who had tried to tell him that there were too many red balls on one side, that they were ruining the balance he was trying to achieve. When he'd gone to the bathroom, I'd corrected the flagrant error in his arrangement of red balls. Just because I was only eight years old didn't mean I had no flair for aesthetic composition. But I paid dearly for my love of beauty, with a rubber hose across my backside that left my buttocks so sore I couldn't sit down for midnight Mass or the rest of Christmas Eve. After he finished turning me into a temporary invalid, he sat down at the Hammond organ and played "O Come All Ye Faithful" and "While Shepherds Watched Their Flocks By Night." My mother ruffled my hair and gave me a handkerchief to wipe the tears and snot off my face and to put an end to my weak protestations, saying, "That's your father," as though to say, "It's God's will," or "That's Stalin for you." God was good in 1951, remember, the Cold War was on and the Korean War not far off. I was eight and at school we were being taught that Communists had big moustaches, dressed badly and were going to wipe us off the face of the Earth with bombs that made mushroom clouds. The little father of the Soviet people was the most dangerous man in the world. The most dangerous man in my world, however, was my father.

HE'S SITTING on the floor, his shoulders covered with an old bathrobe that is so stained and full of holes my mother has been trying to get him to throw it out for the past twenty-five years. He's laughing and waving his hands. It's one o'clock in the morning, but the children are still pulsing with energy. Amandine, my granddaughter, is shouting, and the louder she shouts the louder my father laughs and the more disconcerted my daughter becomes. She doesn't know how to tell her grandfather that her daughter doesn't like him playing with her toys. He's placing, or trying to place, flat wooden crocodiles, lions and sheep into a puzzle from which the same shapes have been cut out with a bandsaw. He fails to do it most of the time, but still seems to be enjoying the challenge. The Banker tells me he's losing his mind, to which I reply that he's having fun. My father takes Amandine's hand and gives her a donkey. She screams even louder. "Please, Grandpa," my daughter pleads. Tears are welling up in her eyes. Sam takes the donkey, whispers something in Amandine's ear, and like all children she switches from fury to delight in a fraction of a second, and falls silent. She sits down, gives the donkey to her great-grandfather and guides his hand to the right cut-out. Then she gives him the lion. He looks at the spaces, tries one, she says no. He tries another and she claps her hands.

Bravo, Grandpa. Now her mother is crying and laughing at the same time. "How do you explain to a little girl that he's her great-grandfather, not her Grandpa?"

"Easy, great-cousin, you tell her to call him Grandpapa."

Sam is proud of his reply. My daughter bursts out laughing. The Tragedienne looks at her son as though seeing him for the first time.

THE SIDEWALK is bare and the weather mild, barely cold. It has been a crazy winter, to the great annoyance of the tourists from France who seem to think Canada was made specifically to provide them with deep snow year-round. The sidewalk is as grey as a tombstone, without even a vague memory of snow. The only suggestions of a White Christmas are a few patches of ice on the cropped lawns of the identical houses, and even they are more black than white. Thirsting for fresh air, I have left the warm bosom of my family. In every house, behind drawn but transparent curtains, shines the same Christmas tree or its double. The same turkey on the same plate of every one of these neighbours who have known each other for years. In France, it's oysters and foie gras. In Cairo, at least in the Westernized houses, it's probably pigeon. Wine, beer and presents everywhere, and people who have no words for the affection they feel for one another but who fiercely and deliberately convince themselves that they are a family, a group, a gang, at least for this one night. Christmas Eve, a harmless invention, the product of a legend the origin of which is a complete mystery. Who knows who started it? Some rebel or fool or visionary calling himself Jesus, the son of God, who scandalized Pharisees, provoked the resentment of many would-be well-wishers whose names we don't know, consorted with a prostitute, had no real father and was therefore the child of a single mother, and a dozen friends. It took twenty centuries for his anonymous birth to become the symbol of family unity. Atheists, Muslims, Taoists, all of us products of churches and consumerism, celebrate Christmas. Humans need to represent themselves, to put on some kind of production, to make theatre. On which side of the stage do I exit least noticeably, backyard or front? I have only a walk-on part, but I want to be believable.

I don't know why I still try to love my father, but I hope these obligatory festivities at least have the appearance of being freely chosen. Maybe I, too, need all this artifice, religious though it be. Maybe I need something that seems permanent, unchanging. And maybe in these times in which we find ourselves the family represents the idea of permanence and continuity, even for the most skeptical among us.

I think of Sam. Yes, he's the one who asked this question, and yes, he has shown by his behaviour that he is a sensitive and intelligent man—no, human being—but how can he possibly understand that at sixty I still want to know why my father stole my walleye? A walleye, a not particularly bright fish that not even fishermen like to catch, in other words a fish that unlike salmon or bass presents no real challenge to the angler and is not even remotely beautiful. A stupid, ordinary fish, except for its delicate flesh, through which the fork slips as through large snowflakes, and which melts on the tongue. My lust for vengeance, which sometimes masqueraded as a passion for justice, has long since evaporated, along with a thousand other childhood sadnesses, leaf by leaf, scattered by the winds of time, which scatters most things. All that remains now is a kind of curiosity about this man who has shaped my life. Why do we want so much to understand Stalin? Perhaps because knowing him will tell us something about our children. And maybe—and I'm beginning to think this might be the case—because if, on the eve of his death, he is suddenly seized by a fit of compassion, perhaps it's because he senses he might have been wrong all his life, that he has failed to understand the mystery of his creator. With a walk-on part, you have to rely on yourself a bit, not just on the principal actor. And there are worse explanations. In Paris last August, more than four hundred elderly people died without their children knowing about it. Killed by the heat in their un-air-conditioned homes, or in rented rooms where no one visited them anymore, or even on the streets, struck down by the stifling sun. I overheard two astonished gendarmes talking to a young daughter and son whose parent had just died, and who were telling the policemen to go fuck themselves. Every night I wondered if my father was dead, and how I would explain to him that in the decay of one human being we see the image of our own future deterioration and that therefore it is always our own suffering we see, never that of the other. No, I came back with Isabelle. It's Christmas and important that we play the Christmas game, even if I no longer have the stomach for it. There are some theatrical productions that we need to see if we are to go on living.

"When did you stop loving your father?" There is only one step between me and the door, and I'm cold. Even if you don't reply to a question, you formulate a response in your head. I think, or at least I have lived according to the belief, that it was when I realized he was the one who made the decisions, who organized me, who told me to smile at the camera when I was squirming to go to the bathroom, it was when I heard him shouting but didn't understand what it was I wasn't supposed to be doing. Did Stalin's children love him? Probably. When he was with them he could allow himself to be generous and warm, because outside the family circle he controlled everything, bestowed the gift of life or death, because nothing was unknown to him and he could feel invincible even in the face of a thousand threats. I don't think that was my father's case. Every time he left the house his certainty did a flip-flop. He had to make a sale, and nothing is less certain than the kind of work that depends for its success on a curious conjunction of seduction and need. He could force me to eat my dinner, he could order me to respect him—or so he thought, his threats had an effect on my mother and on the children. He could intimidate us with his anger. He could dominate us. But outside, he always had to start at square one again being a man of his times. He had to seduce, cajole, argue, compromise. Outside, things were far less certain. This might be an interesting path to take in my exploration of my father, with less wine in me and under different circumstances. But it won't change the fact that I've never loved him. To understand someone is not to love him or even accept him. I could have told all this to Sam, that the truth is I haven't loved my father since I discovered he was my father, the boss, and that he has never loved me. But that would be wrong. The truth is I haven't loved him since I realized I didn't love him.

From a distance I hear the sound of an approaching siren. At the corner of the street I see flashing lights and the cubed bulk of an Emergency-Health ambulance. The vehicle is coming down our street. The front door of the house opens. The ambulance stops in front of me. A gurney emerges through the open doors at the back and two attendants ask me if they have the right address. I say yes, assuming that the Banker wouldn't be shouting from the front steps for no reason.

Another sister calls out: "Dad's dying, there's nothing we can do." All I can do is get out of the way of the attendants and the gurney, and pray that this time he dies. They go in. I don't. I hear them say leave the front door open and the sidewalk clear. My father comes out on the gurney followed by the entire family, most of them supporting my mother, who is crying quietly. There is a mask over his face connected to an oxygen tank, and one of the attendants is massaging his chest above his heart. A sister asks no one in particular how it could be that he found a bag of potato chips. Another voice calls:

"He forgot his teeth!"

"Shut up, everyone!"

I don't know who said that. Sam is sitting on the frost-covered grass with his head down, muttering incomprehensibly.

"Sam's sick, too," cries his mother.

"No, sis, he's just crying."

I walk over to the ambulance and tell the attendants to go. They drive off towards Santa Cabrini, the Italian hospital where my father is a regular customer. It's three blocks away. These days my father goes to hospital as often as I go to a restaurant.

Isabelle asks me what has happened. Nothing. Dad's gone to the hospital. My mother climbed stiffly into the ambulance with the nurse, who practically had to elbow the Homeopath out of the way. The Homeopath apparently thought she, too, should be doing her duty as a daughter and a health professional. Abandoned on the sidewalk, she signals to her husband and he runs to their car, followed by the Banker's partner, who starts the Mercedes and sits in it until the engine warms up (the temperature is about zero) before joining what is beginning to look like a funeral procession. Sam has stopped crying. He stood up when his mother pointedly mentioned the potato chips. His eyes are now so firmly fixed on some distant point in the star-filled sky that he clearly cannot be listening.

I take Isabelle's hand and say, Let's go back inside. From the basement comes the sound of a ping-pong ball and the shouts of the players. My daughter is washing the dishes and her boyfriend is methodically drying them. I don't know who put *Santa Claus is a Louse* on the VCR, but it was an unintentional stroke of genius. Sam's mother is crying softly to herself. Through some bizarre parental transference, she now feels it's her fault that my father got his hands on those potato chips. No, no, it's not your fault if Sam, I mean William, secretly smuggled in chips for him. It was a conspiracy between the two of them. Dad must have insisted, you know what he can be like. He's done the same to you a thousand times, and just because he suddenly can't speak doesn't mean he's lost his powers of persuasion. Julie, however, is unwilling to relinquish her role in the drama. She says through her sobs that Dad snuck one of the bags of chips that Sam had hidden under his bed while he was playing with the children, ate the whole bag, choked on one of the chips, cried out, tried to cough it up but couldn't breathe, and Mother said they had to call 911 and someone did because Mother was panicking.

"He'll only be gone a few hours, you know how crowded those emergency wards are on Christmas Eve."

"But I should have gone with them!" she insists. "We shouldn't have just let them go off while we sit here. Come with me. You're the eldest and it'll make Mother feel more reassured."

"All right," I say, although I know I'd be more useful here helping with the dishes.

We find the tribe huddled together in the emergency waiting room. Only my mother is sitting down. The orange chair they found for her doesn't do much for her colour. She sees me approaching. She seems to have calmed down. No hint of emotion, none of the resignation that comes before imminent death.

"I'm worried because your father doesn't like emergency wards. Last year he was in a corridor on a gurney for two days. He swore at the staff so much they finally found him a bed just to get rid of him. This time he can't talk but he can be pretty unpleasant, even with us. Imagine what he can be like with the nurses. Maybe you should go in there and help calm him down."

I definitely have no desire to go in with my three sisters and two brothers-in-law, but my mother looks at me insistently. How stolid this fragile machine we call the "nuclear family" is. I came here to oblige my sister, and now here I am walking to the reception desk to oblige my mother. I regret it already. The tribal leaders literally have a nurse and doctor surrounded, caught in the family trap. I hang back.

"Yes, madame, I pay taxes, too."

So the Banker has invoked her status as a taxpayer to obtain some service or level of care that the doctor feels is unnecessary.

"Yes, at the time you telephoned he may have been in danger, but not now. The ambulance staff did their job well. His breathing pattern has returned to normal. He vomited a bit, but that's normal at Christmas for a man in his condition. He probably ate too much."

"Have you done an electrocardiogram?"

"No, madame, and we aren't going to do one."

"Because of budget cuts! I knew it! They're sacrificing people's health so they can balance their budget."

"You're absolutely right, madame, but not in the case of your father. There's nothing wrong with him except that he's eighty-six years old, has rigid Parkinson's disease, his heart is exhausted, his arteries are blocked, he's at death's door and he's about as pleasant to deal with as a pit bull. Merry Christmas."

So saying, the doctor exits through the swinging doors leading into the intensive care unit, leaving the exasperated nurse to deal with the tribe. What can you say to a family convinced that their father is dying, the victim of bureaucracy, scientific indifference and, in the case of the Homeopath, medical ineptitude? Nothing, of course. I stay out of it. As does the nurse, who also seeks refuge in the relative calm of the ICU. The Banker follows her into that den of traditional medicine. A few seconds later she reappears, crimson-faced, escorted by two security guards. She splutters in protest, threatens lawsuits, pats her hair and adjusts her enormous breasts as though someone has moved them.

The swinging doors reopen. A burly male nurse enters, pushing a wheelchair with my father in it. Mother fusses, the tribe simpers, and my father smiles like a baby, which is how the elderly smile when they don't have their teeth in. "You go in the taxi with Dad. I'll walk."

THE FAMILY HOME is in a rundown part of the city. Bungalows from the sixties with their pink flamingos on the lawns; rectangular red-brick apartment buildings that have seen better days, garish neon signs, strip clubs, Italian and Haitian cafés eyeing one another competitively, gas stations, dubious storefronts, gangs of stunned youths of all colours haunting the sidewalks, amusing themselves by frightening lone passers-by for a laugh, for kicks, as is the case now with three Haitian rappers blocking my way, forcing me to cross the street and walk on the other side. They laugh, call after me. A thin, cold bead of sweat is running down my back. Fear. I think of my father's impotent rage, but mostly of the shame, that piercing wound, soft, permanent, insidious, of not being or no longer being the image you still have of yourself. Right now I'm ashamed of giving in to those three sad, lost adolescents in their baggy pants. Yes, Dad, it's time for you to die. Not for us, really, because we can get used to your unutterable agony. In fact, by a curious paradox your decrepitude has even drawn us closer together. But it is time you died. Your pride, your dignity, your sense of superiority, your certainty as a provider, everything that has made you what you are, all of it, is being denied you by your illness. And by your family. It must be torture. Worse, it must be humiliating. Why didn't you stuff a few more chips down your throat? "Anatole Lévesque, deceased after an ingestion of vinegar Tostitos, leaves behind his loving wife..." Did your father die after a long illness? No, madame, he ate a bag of potato chips.

MY FATHER is in bed. He told my mother he wanted to sleep. He also wondered why we made him go to the hospital, since no tests were done on him and no medicine was prescribed for him. I'll tell you tomorrow, my mother said, and now, in the family room, she's explaining his reactions. The children are quiet, not out of respect but because they're tired. Some are asleep on the sofas. Amandine is curled up on the carpet beside the Christmas tree, hugging the koala bear that Isabelle and I gave her. Perhaps she's dreaming about having a kangaroo to go with the koala bear. It's two thirty in the morning. The teenagers have gone back to their Donkey Kong tournament. In the family room, the confabulations continue, more serious now. There is no denying the fact that this business with the chips has raised things to a higher pitch. The discussion turns to the possibility of placing my father in a home, which my mother adamantly refuses to consider.

I tell Isabelle that we're leaving, but she signals no. She refuses to let me evade the issue. I do not want to watch yet another family consultation about how my father, whom I don't love, is going to spend the rest of his life.

I feel a hand settle gently on my shoulder. I think it's Isabelle's, but it's Sam's voice I hear.

"Come," he whispers.

We go down to the basement. The chessboard is set up on the ping-pong table. The game has already started; in fact, it's well under way.

"I've been studying it," Sam says. "Look at the positions. The black king is close to being checkmated, but the white queen is under attack. If you look closely, you'll see that the only hope for the king, even if his pawns take the queen, is for White to make some huge gaffe, which seems unlikely. The king could end the game by resigning, accepting his defeat, but kings don't behave that way, not even in chess. So, what's Black's best move?"

All right, I may be slightly drunk but I understand the analogy. I don't know. The options are simple: take the queen even though it's clear that the king is going to die, or kill the king now so he'll stop thinking he's a pawn.

"Grandpa should die," Sam says so quietly I barely hear him.

"Why?"

"Because it would be better for him."

It's not the words or their meaning that explode in my head, because they're the same words I've been thinking myself. It's the tone, the lack of emotion, the firmness, the calm. Like a secretary of state stating why the government has to suppress an innocent citizen because he knows too much, or a doctor pulling a plug without consulting the family. This is a chess player speaking.

"Do you really want to kill my father?"

"No, of course not, what are you, crazy? He's not bothering me. You, maybe..."

"Well then, you don't believe what you just said."

"Yes, I do believe it. Come on, man, don't weird out on me. Take a few deep breaths, as my mother says. I'm not saying we should put a bullet in his brain, or slit his throat, or put a pillow over his face. I don't want to murder my own grandfather. That would change everything, especially him."

"Have you talked to him about it?"

"What? Are you serious? A little twerp like me, talk to my grandfather about his own death? Have you?"

Of course he hasn't talked to my father about it, I tell him, feeling like an idiot. Don't worry about it, he says. We're all idiots when death comes knocking. That's not what he said, but his look pardons my lack of judgement and my confusion. In the ensuing silence neither of us feels uncomfortable because we know we're both thinking the same thing. What do you say to a teenager who asks if you want to kill your father? You have to take him seriously, of course, for his sake, but also for your own. I play through the various options in the chess scenario, but they all come back to the same conclusion. Sam's right. One clear and self-evident thought now paralyzes me and liberates me at the same time. It drowns me like the raging seas that erode the peaceful countryside above the calm beaches and the bay at Paimpol. Sam is right, we have to kill my father. I've known it all along. Ever since I was a child. This death that

I've been hoping for since before I even knew that death was a veritable end, before I knew that death was death, this idea of killing my father, was born in the eternal and mediocre tooth-for-a-tooth. It's the ordinary, pathetic wish of the assassin, to kill something he doesn't understand, as a kind of reflex, the need to eliminate the unknown in his life. Which is why when we are young we kill our fathers, because they punish us, order us about and do not come to our hockey games.

I WAS SEVEN or eight. I remember the details as clearly as though I were watching them on film. I'm wearing a black suit, white shirt and green tie. It's Sunday and we're coming home from Mass. Mother set the table before we left and put the ham-and-pineapple roast in the oven. As soon as we open the door, the children cry out and Mother says, "Good Lord!" Smoke is pouring out of the kitchen, along with a burnt, acrid smell. When my father comes in he starts swearing, something he rarely does. The house is filled with his shouting and cursing. You stupid woman! There is a loud slap and Mother is knocked to the black-and-white tiled floor. One of the white tiles turns red with blood from her nose. And I try to kill my father. I pick up a butter knife from the table and throw myself at him. Now that I think of it, he probably didn't see the knife or understand the significance of my act, the hatred and rage that were so foreign to me but now explode like an atomic mushroom cloud that destroys everything in its path. He slaps me, too, and I find myself on the floor beside my mother. Then, saying he's hungry and he isn't going to settle for just any old thing, he calmly sits down at the piano. My mother gets up and scolds me. A child should never, never hit his father.

She improvised: rice, tomato juice, ground beef and fried onions. It was the kind of meal we usually ate, no one made a fuss about it or even thought about the incinerated ham. Except my father, who took one bite and got up from the table, saying this wasn't a Sunday dinner, he was going to the tavern at the corner where he could get something decent to eat. I squeezed my butter knife. For the second time in an hour I wanted to murder my father.

"NO, I'M NOT like you when you were a kid. I truly want him to die, the sooner the better. I don't want to watch him bawling when I try to tell him about my life. I don't tell him much, just about chess, my teachers, girls, little things. I just want to help him end it. We owe him that."

One thing I can say for certain is that I owe nothing to my father, and Sam owes him even less. We are what we are, especially in this family, with this father who made us parade around like Stalin, keep in step, straight line, forced smiles on our lips, chins high, backs straight, while he made his family propaganda films with his old Kodak movie camera. Neoliberalism has taught us that we don't owe anything to anyone. There, that's me pretending to be an intellectual. The individual creates himself. If he's defective, he'll fail. If nature has made him a genius, he'll rule the world. It was two pure individuals, no one's children, sons of no society, who invented the Mac in a garage that reeked of oil. The celebrities of the week that the tabloids feed on so unimaginatively have faced hurricanes, tsunamis, earthquakes; they have defied prejudice and overcome hurdles beyond belief, and they have done it alone, because they are head and shoulders above everyone else, have thrust their noses above the sea of mediocrity and triumphed over the ordinary. They can go forward, solitary conquerors (because success condemns one to solitude), who make a better future from which we all benefit. That was what I've been trying to explain to this thoughtful teenager. In other words, we owe nothing to the bird whose chirping distracts us from being shot on the field of battle, nor to the wind that refreshes us, nor to the shower that clears our heads after a night of drinking beer. But what a load of crap I'm talking! The very stones owe their existence to the glaciers. I don't know what I owe my father, but it just might be that I owe him his existence. And even if I am nothing but the negative sum of everything he was, it's because of him that I met my mother and my brothers and sisters, because of him I set out on the path that led me to Isabelle. I owe him everything.

"Yes, you owe him a lot, as you say," I tell them.

"It's not rocket science, you know, and most of all it's not killing. Grandma and almost everyone else keeps telling us that two things will kill him, fat and emotions. So we give him both. Lots and lots of fat for cholesterol, and dirty films. We come over, we make a big meal..."

"And watch porno flicks with the two of them after dinner! And the next day the same thing!"

Sam laughs. Stuffing a man with forbidden foods and emotions is not a simple matter. Exactly what emotions does my mother mean when she talks about putting my father's fragile life in danger? We know nothing about his emotions. All we know is how those emotions have been interpreted by his wife, who is our mother and his nurse and his only permanent presence. Why is my mother so insistent about my father's emotions? Is she sending us a hidden message, is she talking about him when he's alive the way we talk about the dead, embellishing them, finding qualities they didn't have and inventing explanations for everything about them that displeased us? Have we been blinded by his authority, his fits of anger and violence? Did we have some secret reason for loving him, known only to her? In any case, why do we need to love someone in order to help him and, in the case of my father, give him this small push into the void accompanied by pleasure and freedom? You don't need to love someone to help him.

Right, then, an apparently simple dilemma: a big meal or a sharp blow to the head, or perhaps an assisted suicide, which would require the complicity of the entire family. And we know how family council meetings drag on and on and never end, like parliamentary committees.

My parents keep cases of beer in the basement and for some mysterious reason never put more than two bottles at a time in the refrigerator in the kitchen, even when they are expecting company, which means their children. No one but us ever visits this house. The last regular guest, one of my mother's cousins, died three years ago. Sam helps himself to a warm beer and brings one for me. He guzzles his as fast as I do mine. I talk to him about the mathematics of gastronomy, and he asks if cholesterol is measured in grams or centimetres. We laugh raucously. We're drinking joyfully, like old friends talking cozily about hockey, which I love, and school, which he hates, but mostly about my wife-to-be, who is much younger than I and whom Sam, blushing, admits to finding attractive. I ask him a few awkward questions, because I no longer know what an adolescent is and I want to find out. He laughs and assures his uncle, each of us with a beer in hand, that yes, he has sex, and to show he's serious he takes a condom from his pocket. We give each other high-fives. Our desire to kill my father, or at least to hustle him along to his death, has put us in a kind of conscious dream-like state. It's like when a voice, a perfect twin of our own, speaks to us just as we are falling asleep, sometimes keeping us awake for hours, making us toss and turn in bed and to curse this voice that is not exactly not our own. Theories and reasons line up like a platoon of soldiers. En masse they are convincing to the most doubting parts of our brains, so much so that in the morning we need to put them into words just to get them out of our heads, down through any passage to the vocal cords, and project them like a sudden spatter of raindrops on the roof for someone, anyone, to hear. Left in the head, words are tremblings, odours, dreads, the construct of dreams or nightmares. But when they surge out through the larynx and into the ears of another, they transform themselves into propositions, proclamations, and suddenly the theatre of the mind is calling up actors. And gestures. There you have it; we are prisoners of our words even if for the moment we prefer to talk about other things.

"May I join your conversation?"

My mother has perfect manners. I don't believe she's ever forgotten a single please or thank you in her life. Sometimes, during meals, she raises her hand like a schoolgirl when she wants to say something. She looks at us with a tender smile that would melt the heart of the most ungrateful child. The mythical smile of the mother, these lips that almost make a heart. We could have said no, and she would gently have asked us to forgive the intrusion. It's not that she lacks will or audacity; on the contrary, she shows respect.

"I don't wish to pry, but what are you discussing?"

"We were talking about Grandpa's death, Grandma."

My mouthful of beer goes down the wrong way, the way designed to take in air rather than liquid, and I choke and splatter my nephew with a fine spray of Boréale Rousse. If looks could kill...

"He's still in good shape, and besides, he doesn't want to die. I might go before he does."

And she gives her tender smile.

"You don't understand, Grandma. We were talking seriously. We're not afraid that he'll die. We want him to. Oh, shit, explain it to her. I don't know how."

My mother looks at me, waiting for her eldest child to speak, her smile now like that of La Gioconda. Serious, full of mysteries that thousands of people have lined up behind Japanese tourists in order to interpret. My mother the painting. I contemplate her. I don't linger over her perfectly coiffed hair, or her golden curls which I've never noticed before but which are pretty and discreet, or over her silk blouse, which is no less discreet and yet acknowledges that she values elegance. Mona Lisa, whom I gave up trying to understand after a dozen visits, is smiling at me. Is it a smile of complicity or defiance? Sam and I have just left a world of superficial thought consisting of elaborate scenarios involving the winning of the lottery, a chance encounter with Jennifer Lopez or ways to rid ourselves of my father. What has she guessed of our intentions, however theoretical they may be? Is she an accomplice or a denouncer?

I know I'm plastered, not just drunk but frankly and joyously pissed to the gills. That must explain why, despite the thorniness of the situation, I remain sitting on the floor, one hand on the ground to give me a certain stability; why I show no emotion, because my neurons are no longer doing the hundred-metre dash but are slogging through the five-thousand-metre sack race trying to come up with an answer that would be close to the one Mona Lisa wants to hear. And then, because my brain is mush, even while I'm wondering what to say I hear my mouth going on a mile a minute. I babble when I drink, I rant, I'm wicked.

Even people who like me and think they know me always describe me with the classic phrase: he didn't know what he was saying. Such people, though I love them dearly, are wrong. Despite a few guilty exaggerations, when drunk I say only what I think. Wine or beer frees me from all the polite restraints and conventions and salaams that society defines as showing tolerance. We will not tolerate intolerance. But when you're plastered, you are not by definition an asshole. You are given more latitude with the truth, a little more leeway. "Go on," says Sam. "Say something." I'm sorry, Isabelle, and so much the worse for me. I slip out of my daydream and into reality.

"All right, Mother, listen. I think it would be better for him and for everybody if we... helped him pass on as quickly as possible."

Mother faints. She falls gently back on the bottom stair, without a sound except that of rumpling silk.

I don't add that it would be all the forbidden food, the wine, the emotions (which ones? I have no idea), the pleasures, what else?—and all that cholesterol, that would be committing the crime. Our role would be more like that of arms dealers, or to put it more diplomatically, facilitators.

Her eyes open, and at the same time she evinces a smile that is no longer Mona Lisa–like but rather one that suggests she has lost her mind, that after the long night's confusion she can't remember a thing. I'm grateful, not only for her swift return to consciousness but also for her apparent amnesia. She says there is no need to mention her fainting spell to the others. They have enough to worry about already.

Right. Three thirty in the morning. Sam and I go back to our conversation. Upstairs, the various families are rounding up their gifts, putting them back in their boxes. Two of my sisters are divvying up the tourtières and the pastries, the orange mousse and what's left of the turkey, as though it all belonged to them. It's like a soup kitchen run by civil servants, everyone gets an equal portion of everything whether they want it or not. The eyes of the children look like those of children in fairy tales after the Sandman has been and gone. The older ones are impatient to be home. They hug each other absently. Everyone pays lip service to the old rituals. Mother, a little shakier than usual, like a wounded sparrow left out in the winter cold, is smiling and hugging everyone and wishing them well and making encouraging comments. A machine dispensing affection, a little old lady who is stronger than Stalin and all the other dictators put together. Isabelle kisses her. They are great friends, these two. My mother whispers something in her ear, and Isabelle turns and looks at me without smiling, her eyes brimming with questions. I hug Mother and she tells me, as she almost always does, to look after Isabelle, smoke and drink a little less, and come visit her more often. Sam takes my arm as he goes out. He'll call me tomorrow. When words leave the brain, they need gestures and actors to attach themselves to. Sam's seem to belong to a play I haven't seen, though I know how it ends.

I sober up. I repeat: words are fragmentation bombs. I sober up even more.

FINALLY, IT'S snowing. It's like one of those old Christmas cards, with enough space between the feathery flakes to see the stars in the sky, especially the most brilliant of them (which I think is Venus), which once guided the wise men to the stable. Did they travel on dromedaries or camels with two humps? I can't remember all the figurines in a crèche anymore. Isabelle drives slowly, humming a tune I don't recognize, a haunting, nostalgic melody slowly unfurling its inflections like large sails in a warm wind. I place it: it's a song sung by Fairouz, the Lebanese diva who has so enchanted the Arabs except for certain fundamentalists who prefer their own throaty, venomous sermons. It feels good to let my thoughts stray from their wanted haunts. I try going back to the old Arab Quarter in Rabat and the tajine I ate with my daughter in the chic Hilton restaurant, the time she climbed up on the stage with the belly dancers and danced with them, me not knowing what to do and the other customers laughing and the Moroccan women leading her through a sweet, sensual saraband. I am almost there.

"Is it true you want to kill your father?"

She spoke softly. I sensed no reproach in her voice, but I'd rather be in Rabat than at the corner of Park and Bernard, stopped at a red light in a car that smells of tourtière and doughnuts we'll probably end up throwing out.

"No, Isabelle, I don't. It's more complex than that."

"Well, that's what your mother thinks. I just thought I'd warn you."

Damn. So she does remember.

IN OUR FAMILY, PRESENTS HAVE ALMOST
ALWAYS HAD TO DO WITH EITHER THE TABLE
OR THE KITCHEN. A TRAVELLER (WHO, IN OUR
family, travels to the south of France) brings us a Provençal tablecloth or, if he or she has blown the budget on restaurants, a set of napkins in the same intense yellows and
blinding blues, crawling with cicadas. The Buddhists give
100 per cent organic produce: farm-gate lavender honey, a
cassis liqueur from plants unsullied by pollution, truffle-
flavoured olive oil that some one-eyed rustic in Périgord
has been making for the past fifty years. Gifts from the
Medicals tend to be sauternes or plum brandies, lightly
cooked foie gras, pots of goose confit, vintage Arma-
gnacs. Strange. And to go with the napkins, adherents
to both philosophies give hand-turned ceramic serving
plates, designer pepper mills, Italian-made salad bowls and
spoons, and each year a new kind of container for keeping
soft drinks once they're opened, the one this year being
designed to accept those new plastic corks that are popping

up everywhere, even from the better vintners, to replace cork, which is becoming rarer and rarer because humanity has drunk too much wine and replanted too few oaks.

Despite the fact that Isabelle has moved into my apartment, it still has something of the old bordello about it. In the room we're sitting in now there are stacks of records and books in the corners, newspapers lying about, an old defunct candelabra that I rescued from a stage set. It was much worse before she moved in. Eleven months ago she came, having been accustomed to order, harmony, a decor straight out of *Elle* magazine, and she didn't say a word. Three days later she'd washed all the floors and windows, which I had been neglecting for months. In the reflection of a new lamp on the dark, gleaming floorboards, I rediscovered the beauty that my laziness and indifference had allowed to become a pigsty. Bit by bit but relentlessly, like a cat staking out its territory, she hung a painting here, replaced a table there, put a vase on it that somehow miraculously sprouted flowers, bought plates and glasses, napkins and a duvet, still without saying a word, never asking my opinion or expecting any approval or thanks. Since her taste was impeccable, I, too, said nothing, secretly hoping, lazy bastard that I am, that she would take on the entire apartment, get in bookshelves, get rid of all my chipped and stained furniture, and why not buy me some new clothes while she was at it, my years of bachelorhood having imposed a kind of accidental poverty upon me? All I owned were two pairs of jeans, two pairs of shoes and a few shirts.

I now feel more and more myself in this apartment, and in these clothes she buys me.

We make an inventory of the gifts over which I gushed and said thank you and bestowed kisses during the family exchange. What does one do with a miniature bottle of rose-petal vinegar? I twist off the tiny cap and sniff the faint mimicry of a flask of perfume sold on the Internet. It smells like vinegar to me. Isabelle agrees. And this decanter, our tenth. Isabelle smiles. It will be our eleventh vase. A bottle of madiran, the celebrated Château Montus de Brumont. Now that's a gift! From Bernard. Isabelle, who has loosened her hair, produces two teacups, a gift from some unknown amateur, it would appear, of Oriental motifs. The house of Brumont will surely pardon the cultural hybridization.

"So is it true you want to kill your father?"

Her tone hasn't changed, the volume hasn't shifted a decibel either way, but that could betray an insistence, the urgency of her need to know. I know Isabelle. I'll get no sleep tonight unless I give her an answer. The Brumont is nearly black, like blood coagulating in the wound of a bull. Or like my father's blood, thick and dark, rising ever more slowly to his brain.

I try to explain everything that has been going through my mind throughout the evening, and gradually, as sobriety returns thanks to the madiran, it all comes back to me.

"My father is dying hating himself and hating the world. We are keeping him alive while he is preventing us from living. We're struggling for our mutual unhappiness. There was a time when we laughed uproariously, as he did, when food fell off his fork and like a child he would say, 'Oops, dropped it.' He'd pick it up and try again and smile at our enthusiastic applause when he succeeded in getting it to his mouth. We did everything but cry *Encore!* That was before we or he knew about all those enzymes and whatever other chemicals were working like anarchists' secateurs in his brain, blindly snipping away at the flowering vines of his neurons. We thought we were watching and taking part in a convalescence that would slide gently towards a normal death, one that would come in its own time, like a season, or a gentle rain that we knew was coming because we'd heard the weather reports. But we are not watching a convalescence; we're participating in a degeneration, a slow, methodical, implacable wasting away. We wanted to do the right thing, but as George Bush's inspector said about the weapons of mass destruction, we were wrong. We accept the inevitability of his imminent death, but we aren't prepared for the ugliness or more particularly the relentlessness of his suffering, or for the consequences it's having for my mother. We thought my father would die decently, without disturbing anyone, pass away in his sleep, perhaps, which would have been perfect, or else go the way the statistics say he's supposed to go: have a second stroke, spend a few days in the hospital, we get a phone call early one morning and there's a funeral where we shed a few tears and tell ourselves we've done our duty by him. We thought death would come like a thief in the night. Unfortunately for him, for my mother and to some extent for us, the thief didn't take his sackful of silver and bugger off; he seems to have liked the place and decided to move in.

"Now when he tries to get up from his chair, equipped though it is with a motor that would lift him up and practically set him down on the floor, some of us turn away and others of us watch in irritation because he refuses to use the damned motor. What an idiot, wanting to stand up without help from a few springs hidden in the cushions. How thoughtless of him, the ingrate. But would we feel the same way about a general who wanted to stand unsupported before his troops even when he's mortally wounded? And then there's the pleasure. Because it's the absence of pleasure or even happiness that's his worst agony. If only he could complain about an unbearable pain hacking away at his brain or tearing at his insides or torturing his muscles, but no, he doesn't need sleeping pills or painkillers, he doesn't suffer any physical pain, there is no drug that could bring him the pleasure of relief. There is only the sharp, shooting pain of the soul, the crippling of awareness, the unspeakable pain. Can we even imagine Stalin's shame when he dropped that vodka bottle in front of the Central Committee, and got down on the red carpet on his hands and knees to pick it up? And Comrade Khrushchev barely leaning over to offer his arm, and Molotov looking away? We are Dad's politburo. His powers are abandoning him, and for men like him power is the only pleasure.

Tell me, Isabelle, what happiness is there in my father's life that justifies our prolonging it? Is it perhaps the pleasure of watching others live? Is it like watching a movie?"

"No. How are you going to do it? No, don't go silent on me. Tell me. What exactly are you planning to do?"

"Not me, actually, Isabelle. Or not only me. There's Sam. All I do is talk, put thoughts into words, and Sam, who isn't old enough to shave yet, translates them into actions. That's more or less what's happening. Sam and I had come to the same conclusion before we even talked about it and from completely different perspectives. I was thinking about the pleasure of living, and Sam was surely more concerned with the pleasure of dying. Perhaps we can poison him"—I cannot bring myself to say *kill*—"by letting him eat. He can still eat, stuff himself, belch, flush with pleasure after a forbidden slice of Reblochon cheese. When he eats he's still alive. That's all there is to it, really. I'd rather he died than went on living."

Isabelle smiles. She takes my hand and, still smiling, walks me through a rehearsal of my father's death. "We'll start with some foie gras," she says, laughing now, shaking with mirth as I open one of those conserves that are sold in Roissy in boutiques that are no longer duty-free and that charge twice what you'd pay in an ordinary supermarket for a tin of duck-liver mousse spiced with a hint of truffle. She is speechless with laughter. She signals, gestures, chokes with chuckles mixed with wine, which is astonishing in someone as well brought up as she has been. She points to herself, stabs her chest with her finger. She stamps her feet on the hardwood floor, probably awakening the downstairs neighbour, who will no doubt have something scathing to say about it tomorrow.

"For your father..." She takes a breath. "That was my present for your father."

We blew our chance to kill him.

IT'S BOXING DAY AND MY FATHER HAS
STARTED GOING TO DAY HOSPITAL. DAY HOS-
PITAL IS FOR ADULTS WHAT DAY CAMP IS FOR
children. Day camps have been around for a long time. Parents who have to work during school holidays drop their
kids off with activity leaders, or hired guards called moni-
tors, and in principle the kids are there to have a good time.
They play sports, surf the Internet, eat in cafeterias where
they gorge themselves on calories, are taken to swimming
pools to work them off, and at the end of the day are picked
up by parents exhausted after a day at work. The reunions
are always joyful. Day hospital is a more recent phenome-
non but is modelled on the same formula. It's a way for the
parent living at home to get a break, to go out and do the
shopping without having to worry about what the aged
child left in the family home is up to. The aged child can be
dropped off at day hospital, ostensibly to get care; he is
given tests, asked impertinent questions about the colour
of his bowel movements, left to fester in waiting rooms

because the system is overused, taken to eat in cafeterias, where he gorges himself on calories, is not taken to swimming pools but speaks to doctors and waits for hospital staff members to herd him more or less gently onto a little bus, which takes him home. The reunions are not always joyful.

When my mother called yesterday, she did not speak with her usual delicacy or nuance. She normally starts by asking me for details of my daily life, tells me what's on television that day, describes my father's latest fall, asks after Isabelle and raises the possibility that I might come for a visit, if and when I have the time, no hurry. This time it's "Come tomorrow afternoon. There's still some tourtière left and I need to speak to you. No, don't bring any more wine, there's plenty here."

A PRETTY CHILD of five or six with what looks like a daisy stuck in her curled hair. It's my mother—I recognize her by her look, soft and sparkling at the same time. She's smiling at the camera while behind her a gaggle of children are running about in an immense garden. You can see a few adults here and there in the background, men in black suits with ties or cravats around stiff collars. And farther off, almost like shadows, a few women. The garden must be flowing with mischievous laughter and tears and shouts, since that's what gardens are like on Sundays when a dozen children are playing in them after Mass and before dinner, those two intolerable brackets in the day of a child who knows instinctively that you don't learn much about life when you're sitting or kneeling. The men—there are three of them—are paying no attention to the women nor to the swarm of offspring they've brought into the world. Your grandfather, my mother says, pointing to the photograph, your great-grandfather, she says to Sam, who gave me a look when I came in that told me I didn't know what I was in for, and who goes on looking at the dozens of photographs lined up purposefully on the teak table in the living room.

A pretty child with many sisters and brothers, all of whom look as wise and well brought up as she. Unlike the usual photo albums delineating the history of respectable families, this one contains no pictures of her sitting at a piano, or reciting poetry on a stage beside a cardboard tree. But there she is holding a rosary, kneeling before the statue of a Christ who seems to be bleeding profusely, or standing with a group of nuns. As she approaches adolescence there seem to be more and more Masses and religious ceremonies, she dressed in black and minus the daisies in her hair, her smile now little more than a thin line and the sparkle of her gaze hidden behind the veil of her eyelids, impenetrable barriers between herself and the camera that might otherwise have revealed her inner thoughts. Of course she makes no comment. She has gone into the kitchen to reheat the tourtière and mash the potatoes, to keep herself busy while the thread of her life unravels on the teak table. I'm the one trying to give some meaning to the photos, while Sam expresses disbelief about the ridiculous clothing people wore on whatever planet his grandmother grew up on. Sam, has no one ever told you at that school of yours that there was a time before digital cameras when photographs came in black and white and, before that, in sepia, and that in those days clothing wasn't something designed to exhibit the belly buttons of ten-year-old girls? How old is she in this one? Sixteen, seventeen? Now even the thin line of her smile has disappeared, the left hand rests in the right just above the hip, and the eyes are looking at nothing, reduced as they are to dull pupils and irises. My grandfather, whom I never knew, is standing behind her with his large hands on her shoulders. He is staring intently at the camera, defying it to try stealing any part of himself, smiling paternally behind his Stalinesque moustache. Is it a smile or a rictus? Is that why some men, especially dictators, grow thick moustaches, so that they can do for the lips what eyelids do for the eyes? And here is my mother's favourite brother, on the arm of a young woman who appears to have some class, as they say, and her older sister smiling at someone who seems to be a nice guy, a bit of a paunch, a tad dapper, with that handsome innocence that comes with baby fat. The more people there are around her, all smiling broadly, their dresses becoming lighter and lighter, some of the men wearing neither jackets nor ties, the more serious she herself looks. Yes, Sam, I am making this up, interpreting the photographs, trying to read past the outward signs, to see through the old clichés. Why don't you just ask her? She wouldn't answer. I don't know if that's true or not, but I could never put these questions

to her. A son who asks his mother about her love life is trying to undress her. Besides, the answers are right here in
front of us, in these photos. Here's a wedding picture. It
was a big wedding. Look at this series taken from behind by
someone with an automatic camera standing in the central
aisle of the church. All those backs, and the priest standing in the middle speaking to a white back and a black back.
Those are her curls, under that white pillbox hat with the
flower stuck in it, fourth row on the right. And to her left a
man whose back I don't know. He towers head and shoulders above her. Here's the same man looking at her, Mother
hiding a smile with one hand while holding her hat on with
the other. We can see how windy it is, because the man is
trying to keep his Brylcreemed hair from flying about. He's
not smiling. He has a thin moustache that makes a black
smudge under his aquiline nose. He seems out of place.
That's my father taking his first steps into the middle class.
He looks cool, Sam exclaims, at least for those times. I
hear my mother setting the table in the kitchen. How's it
going in there, children? We murmur fine, which she probably can't hear. It's always summer, always the same garden. The blacks and whites become better separated, show
more detail. Kodak must have put a new generation of film
on the market. The men in their stiff collars have not aged
at all since the photo in which my mother was seven. They
had already done their aging by then, and have remained
obstinately the same age, as though they had been born
as statues. They talk implacably, heedless of the changes

taking place around them. My mother sitting on a see-saw, waiting for my father to send her up with a single, virile push. But he stands stiffly behind her, like a prisoner in his checked suit, as though trying to seem as old as the others and wondering if any display of enjoyment would upset the family he has just become a part of. Him, a product of diabetes, obesity, poverty and vulgarity.

Another wedding picture, this one also a classic. My father and mother's official wedding portrait, the couple having just been united by God for better or for worse until they are dead, as they say of someone about to be hanged. A hundred people lined up on the steps in front of the church, like rows of onions. I put my finger on certain faces, for Sam. The great-grandfathers and great-grandmothers, the uncles and aunts. The bourgeoisie and their offspring, united for a festive celebration that will not take place again. Of all these grey faces, my mother's beams the most. My father wears a small smile, unless that's just the effect of his moustache or the negative is blurred. And here's me. I recognize this one, me in my mother's arms. She's still smiling. With each photo there are more of us, we surround her, multiple images of her with the same smile on her face, although it never seems forced. By the time colour film arrives there are five of us, a baby every eighteen months on average. After the sixth there is a photo that seems incongruous: a large yellowish fish on the kitchen table beside a trophy that has the figure of a fisherman making a shallow cast.

"Sam, that's my walleye."

Naturally he doesn't understand.

The children behave like children and my mother looks radiant. In the shots in which there are nine of us, the Director has solved the problem of symmetry by placing the smallest in the front row, on their knees, my mother in the middle of the second row with two children on either side of her and the ninth, me, the eldest, standing behind her. Symmetry comes naturally to Dictators, since it both represents and perpetuates their view of the world. Long before his madness allowed him to imagine himself as führer, Hitler painted careful, meticulous watercolours, perfectly framed; he later ordered Speer, his favourite architect, to build fortifications scrupulously inspired by Greek symmetry; what he liked best about Leni Riefenstahl's films was her geometric depiction of ceremony. When Stalin watched his people, which is to say his army, march before him, what did he see? Long rectangles, compact squares, composed of thousands upon thousands of identical figures with even the tips of their noses sighted along an imaginary line. It might be thought that my father's subsequent passion for the home-movie camera would introduce an element of disorder, and therefore of realism, into the family photograph, which had hitherto existed as proof of our exemplary behaviour. Not so. Though armed with a tool capable of recording movement, my father persisted in filming still photographs. And when sound came on the scene he developed a sudden aversion for movie making altogether. Of course he could have simply ordered us to be silent and immobile and we would have obeyed, but there were birds, children shouting in the streets, ambulance sirens, chaos, real life, all destroying the symmetry of the image.

"Lunch is served."

What are we meant to see in this photographic biography of my mother? What does she want us to discover there? Is she trying to show us that she's happy? Why not just say it, Mother: I'm happy? I suppose mothers of her generation don't say such things. They work through detours and allusions, they aren't given to direct statements. When she wanted to know if I needed money, she would say something about my clothes. Was I wearing these faded old jeans because I liked them? And before I could answer she'd observe that the kind of people I hung out with seemed to just wear any old thing. But couldn't I use a new pair? Unless I swallowed the hook whole and confessed that I could use a small loan, my last play hadn't done that well and that very morning at 6:00 am the landlord had phoned to demand his pound of flesh. And as if by magic an envelope full of money would appear before me.

MY MOTHER IS smiling the smile of the photos. And nibbling. Sam is wolfing. As for me, I'm waiting for some anodyne phrase to indicate the gentle road down which the conversation will unfold. At the moment she's talking about chess, wondering if one can make a living at it, raise a family on the money a workforce of pawns could bring in. Sam hasn't clued in that what she's saying is that she wants him to study hard and go to university. He's all excited, talking about the fabulous sums Fischer and Kasparov are raking in. But what if you're not Bobby Fischer? Sam frowns slightly.

"Are you happy, Grandma? And is Grandpa?"

He has tossed in a grenade, like a terrorist who has given careful thought to the matter. His tone is even, no trace of emotion.

"Would you like some dessert?"

"No."

"What about you?"

"Me neither."

Mother is still smiling, but her eyes have become veiled and her eyelids flutter nervously.

"Coffee?"

"No."

"Grandma, were you always as happy as you are in those photos?"

Grandmothers never lie to their grandchildren unless to protect them from life. And grandchildren believe less and less of what their grandmothers tell them. Life is handed to them in spades in their first school textbooks, which are about all the things their parents display and lug about in their permanent reality show. Parents don't shield their children from their own unhappiness anymore. In my mother's day, unhappiness was hidden, or rather never named. Unhappiness had no name, any more than happiness did. Happiness was duty, which was also unhappiness.

Mother looks down and sighs, the knife she's holding in her left hand making tiny clink, clink, clinks on the edge of her plate. Her right hand reaches over and rests on the left, to stop its trembling. The knife is quiet. No, she has not always been as happy as that, but what's more important, she says, is that she has no regrets. She is proud of her life. She rests her little bird's head on her fragile shoulders and is Edith Piaf singing *Non, rien de rien, non, je ne regrette rien.*

"So you wish to kill my husband because you think he's not happy. Perhaps you should ask him what he thinks about that. We don't kill the people we love without asking their permission, even if we think we're doing them a favour."

Do you know the expression "You could hear a fly flying"? I can hear the fly. And it isn't even flying, it's walking. The silence is so heavy I can hear it chomping on the cheese we're not eating. Everything depends on how it's stated. So, you want to kill my husband. It makes us sound like assassins, or worse, like disrespectful children because we haven't consulted with the victim. She's right. We must ask him how he feels about all this. We're talking about death here, no small thing. I try to imagine it. Dad, do you want to die? He chokes, nearly dies choking, and bursts out with a roar, No, turning beet red. Well, then, Dad, do you want to go on living like this for a long time? He doesn't understand what "like this" means. Without being able to read? No. Without being able to eat what you like? No. Without being able to speak? No.

Without being able to live? He would probably say Yes. Bloody hell, Dad, do you know what you're saying? You want to live without living? Yes, he says, as pigheaded as ever. He laughs. I'm bringing him into the discussion, but we're not talking to each other. Why do you want to live? He laughs. Because. That's exactly what he would say, I'm sure of it: Because. Which is the answer children give.

I'VE JUST HIT my sister. Her bottom lip is bleeding slightly. I'm ten, she's six. My father takes my arm and shakes me like a dishrag. Why did you hit her? I don't like her. Why not? Because. He hits me, of course, and a lot harder than I hit my sister. But I clench my teeth and do not cry. Why? Because. Because I don't want to say I don't know, I don't want to show my ignorance and confusion. Because.

BECAUSE I EXIST and must go on existing, as Stalin and my father would answer. I'll never ask my father if he wants to die. I listen to the fly walking across the sugar bowl. I take a deep breath, as William's mother says, William who would rather be called Sam and who is thinking as he chews his fingernails.

"We were joking, Mother. Not joking exactly, but we were just talking off the tops of our heads. I'd had a lot to drink... and we were just wondering if Dad was getting any pleasure out of living, and whether—"

"Whether I wouldn't be happier without him, as you would be, perhaps?"

"No, Grandma. We weren't joking and we don't want to kill Grandpa, we just want him to die. There's a difference. We were saying that we had to help him. Not, like, push him down the stairs or anything, not kill him, Grandma, just, fuck, I don't know how to put it, just... just help him leave."

Words are a prison. If you want freedom, no responsibilities, don't talk. I know that if it weren't for Sam's intervention I'd have found a way out of this, my mother and I would have entered a kind of shadow world where we could have gone on for a long time without evoking the dark thoughts that dwell within each of us. That's how she and I have been living for a while now, in a sort of unspoken acceptance that we thought would slowly relax into forgetfulness. Now there is nothing holding us together, Sam, my mother and me. Sam loves his grandfather, and leading him joyously to his tomb is a kind of kiss on the forehead. Mother is long past the age of love. She accepts a destiny that dictates a duty, a destiny she has chosen and a duty that her faith demands. I do not love my father. I feel nothing for him but pity. Except that pity is not a feeling, it's the complacency of the weak. I don't want revenge, I'm past that. I only want him to disappear, for my mother's sake, for the family's sake, so that we can change the subject of all our conversations, so we can have Christmas dinner without rancour, so we no longer have to listen to him refuse to have an operation to prevent him from going blind. I envision a civilized death for him as a result of a superabundance of pleasure, from an embolism caused by cholesterol, or a tumble after drinking a bottle of Puligny-Montrachet. But I know it's not for his sake I want him to end his days happily; it's only out of laziness. I want to kill him without killing him. Above all, afraid of death as I am, I would like to give him the death I want for myself. Gentle, quick, painless. As for my mother, we can only imagine—no, invent how happy she would be without my father. There are two possible scenarios. In one, she's exhausted, fed up with not being allowed to leave the house, terrified every time he falls because she cannot lift him on her own, wonders what he'll be like when he's blind, wonders even more what she'll be like. That's one way to interpret her words. But there's another reading. That of the friend who has come to be both nurse and mother, the one who describes, sometimes wearily, the state of the patient. If she spares us no detail, it's not because she's complaining, she's merely acting out of her sense of professionalism or duty. Maybe she's telling us that this is her destiny, that she would prefer a gentler one, perhaps, but she accepts the hand she's been dealt, and maybe playing it out has become her reason for living. Is that what she is telling us?

"It would be better for my husband if he were dead. For his sake, that is what I think, but also for everyone else's, for me, for you. But he doesn't want to die. I've talked to him about it. He sees you and he feels happy. He sees this house and he feels proud. He remembers and sees his memories marching and eating before him."

My mother retracts her wet bird's head into her shoulders as though she thinks she has said too much. Sam turns pale. I have found a way out.

"We forget, Sam, that—"

"Yes, we forget, I know, but I often see him crying when I tell him what I'm doing."

"I see him cry, too, William. He cries because he can't hear Céline Dion talking about sick children, because he can't see the puck when he watches hockey on TV, because he disgusts you during meals, because he can't hear what you're saying and he doesn't have time to answer before you answer for him. He cries ten times a day. At first it made me feel terrible. My husband, crying! And I tried to console him, as I would comfort a baby who can't tell me where the pain is coming from. I can't tell you how much anguish and torment I suffered because I didn't know how to calm him when he cried like a baby. But I'm used to it, now. Tears are just another thing to wipe away, like spit or snot. It's part of his illness. So I wipe them away. I know you are kind. I assume that your conversations are crazy but they are only meant to relieve me, and maybe to give him some pleasure, but for now it isn't my husband who is killing me, it's life, your lives spinning around ours. My husband and I have been eating margarine for thirty years, and now we're told that our arteries are blocked and we should have been eating butter. The cardiologist lectures me about the fat in salmon, the psychologist tells me not to worry about any of it, and you, my children, watch us as though we're animals in a cage, discussing our diets and our emotions and trying to convince me that this is best or that is better. A mother's problem, William, is that she wants to make everyone happy. Not even God can do that. Pour me a small glass of wine... And my husband is dying. Of course I'll be happy for him when he finally goes, even though he doesn't want to die. I'll be sad, but I won't be unhappy. I'll rest for a week, you'll come over nearly every day, and I'm not sure I want to leave this house but I do know that I would rather talk to my husband who doesn't answer me than to the four walls that don't hear me. I might start doing volunteer work, but who would I talk to about that? You, I suppose, during your rare visits, or on the telephone, to fill the time between visits, but good lord, your lives are so full, what with children and projects and debts and divorces and mistresses, you're all so busy living that I feel like a stranger with my ordinary little corner of life. And my arteries are already hardening and they're going to get harder and eventually the doctors and you children will get hold of me. You'll take my fate in your hands. William will visit me and bring me bags of potato chips and his mother or one of his aunts will be scandalized, and you, my son, you'll write a play in which a son wants to kill his mother to liberate her from her sad and lonely existence... I'll have some coffee with a little brandy in it, please, there's a bottle under your father's bed... brandy wakes me up when

I've had some wine... I think I'm a little tipsy... I'm going to have a nap until your father comes home..."

She smiles coolly, like a cat asking permission to go on biting an outstretched finger. She isn't really looking at us, she's settling her gaze on us for a fraction of a second. Then, taking a deep breath that produces a slight groan, she continues.

"Why doesn't my husband want to die? His life is an intolerable burden to him. Why don't I want to die, even though I'm so exhausted, so, so tired? Because we're afraid. Yes, even though we're good Catholics, we're afraid there's nothing else, nothing after death. There, I've said it."

She pours herself a good dollop of brandy and explains that duty is a form of affection, life is an obligation that comes from God, and the sight of children whether happy or sad is what pushes us to go on. If they're happy, then it cheers and reassures those who are about to die; if they're sad, then they are someone we can give comfort to, they give us the will to endure so we can be there when the sadness comes back. That's why we go on living when life is disappearing. Because a new life is being born. Of course she's only speaking for herself, and she very much doubts that my father entertains the same thoughts. To tell us the truth, she doesn't know why he torments himself, because that's what he's doing, she's convinced of it.

"Do you remember the walleye in the photo, how proud he was of it? He waved the trophy around and called the neighbour over to make him jealous of his prize. I remember your silence, and how you wouldn't touch a mouthful of it when we ate it to celebrate your father's victory, even though you normally liked fish. He was in a foul mood that night, and I didn't know why. He loved winning so much. And then he told me that he had stolen the fish from you. He didn't want to be embarrassed by his own son. I can tell you this now, he wasn't proud of it. Do you remember that fish? Can you imagine his humiliation? If it were me I would have wanted to die. There we all were, standing around him like nurses, or policemen, or judges, even his great-grandchildren. 'Look out, Grandpa!' No, I couldn't have done it, but I don't have the right to think as you do. But maybe it would be a good thing if we went together... to death, maybe it would... Okay, I'm going to have a nap. No need to tidy up, there's not a lot going on around here."

She gets up. She is stooped, not with the burden of years but with the weight of words and thoughts, so many words, so many thoughts in such a small, curly head that once, as a child, dreamed in a garden filled with old people. But what was she really dreaming of? A garden of daisies, perhaps?

"Mother, what did you dream about when you were a child?"

"A big house and a husband and a lot of children. There, you see? Despite what you call my modernism, I'm not so different from most women of my generation. You make me out to be a beauty because you think your father is a beast.

But he saved me from the convent, which is where my family would have sent me."

The doorbell rings and my mother, surprised, says the mailman has already been by. She hurries to the door and peeks out from the vestibule. She cries out in alarm.

"It's your father. There must be a problem."

Yes, there's a problem all right. My father is sitting in a wheelchair imprisoned in a straitjacket. Two male nurses are standing with him, one on either side, looking fed up. My mother is indignant, and so is William, who comes up and puts an arm around her shoulders. "My husband is not a madman, you have no right." The nurses protest mildly. They've seen it all before. My father lost his temper. When a nurse tried to take a blood sample he grabbed the syringe from her and stabbed her with it. Then he started shouting, which is why he is gagged. They try to explain, but explanations are not part of their job description, they are not officially required to say anything except the day-hospital administration has decided that this gentleman has behaved in a way that posed a threat to the other patients and hospital personnel. My mother begins to shake, goes up to him and takes his hand, which he pulls away. He looks angry and hard, the way he used to look after whipping me with his belt, his eyes cold and grim at the same time because of the ferocity of my punishment and the seriousness of the situation.

"We've given him something to calm him down, ma'am. He wouldn't stop shouting, he kicked anyone who got too close to him, he spat at them, yes, he spat on me. All he would say was Enough, and Stop. You never know how old people are going to react."

My father is shivering, and so are we. We all feel the same chill. It isn't much, but it's something. William removes the gag. I brace myself for the shouting and complaining, but no, there's only the icy silence of the day after Christmas when the sun glints off the snow and blinds us mortals. My father begins to shiver more violently. His teeth chatter and his head shakes, and I realize he is naked under his thin green johnny-shirt. I hadn't noticed it before because of the straitjacket covering the upper half of his body. I look at his ugly, deformed legs, wooden sticks poking out of the cloth like obscene flotsam.

It's warmer in the kitchen. The straitjacket has been taken off. He has a blanket over his shoulders and we are sitting at the table, waiting for him to say something. Nothing comes. The look in his eyes hasn't changed, it's the look of a man who has come to a decision. Mother keeps pumping him for answers. He lifts a cup of coffee to his lips with a sure hand; Mother is ready with a napkin but he transfixes her with a look that says, Not this time. He puts the cup down like a normal person. He reaches for Mother's hand, then changes his mind.

"E...nough...stop...die. I want to die."

He picks up the cup, his hand still steady. Mother releases her breath and lowers her eyes. William says, Shit. And me? I don't want to be here. When Mother begins to murmur as though she were rocking a cradle—Oh my husband, what are we doing? Oh my husband, what are we doing?—it's all I can do to keep from jumping up and running out of the house. I don't want to hear this. I'm only here by accident, because of some dream that got put into words. I'm a hostage of my own imagination. If I express myself in words, it's because I want to say something, to tell something, not so I can get caught up in my own discourse. Staging a play is a way of organizing a life we refuse to share, and art today is rarely anything but an escape. A wife, her sense of responsibility, the exaltation and fear of having to live alone. No, ever since my father began beating me, that is precisely what I have refused to take part in. I wasn't responsible for the violence, typical though it was for the time, and so I decided not to be responsible for anything. Not out of fear of being punished, but out of fear of having to pay the price. I therefore refused to take part in any activity that produced a tangible, measurable result, whose product could be the subject of objective evaluation. I refused to be judged, because if I am not judged I cannot be punished. Creativity exists outside the rational grid of judgement; it's a bomb shelter for the weak and the anxious, the tormented and the clairvoyant. A bad play is not a mistake, it's a pathway to an interesting exploration. And there's always someone around who adores your worst work, some introvert who writes to you saying you've released her from her iron collar, or a WASP couple who send you a we-don't-know-if-we-should-accept-or-refuse-your-challenge-do-we-love, while waiting to read the reviews before making up their minds. A doctor doesn't have such leeway, can't afford to be complacent about botching a childbirth or an operation on a brain tumour. Nor can the cop when he draws and fires and finds out later that what the man in the dark alley was pointing at him was an over-ripe banana. I chose to invent my own universe, at least until Isabelle came along, somewhat late in my life, to draw me slowly into reality, which is where I am now because of my words, my spoken dreams, and because of William and my father, whom I now love for the first time because he hollered "Stop!" My mother coughs and puts a hand on my arm.

"Son," she says quietly, "you could write a play about both of us having a good death."

"Yeah!"

The sound is pure relief, joyful and raging. My father bursts out with a laugh mixed with choking and gagging. William's eyes widen, Mother finds her Mona Lisa smile again, Dad gets his breath back, barely, and shouts:

"A good death!"

And smiles. For the first time in years I don't notice his toothless mouth; all I see are his lips forming a real smile.

"I'm starving!"

He laughs again and places a hand on my mother's shoulder, and she senses immediately that it's a new hand, or rather the old hand, the hand from the garden, the hand from their first days together. She leans her head to the right so that her cheek touches the transformed hand. An old person's muscles are not designed for acts of love or affection. A few curls tickle the back of my father's hand, but her tired, stiff neck prevents the cheek from resting on the hand that remains on her shoulder and looks soft. I could be imagining this. I could be wrong. My father is not Stalin, he's a weak dictator, stripped of all his certainties. His violence spoke only of his weakness and his fear of life. His hand slides slowly from her shoulder to her arm, the way mine does with Isabelle, stops on her forearm for a few seconds and then settles on her hand. It's the gesture of discothèques and bars, a creature of shadow and noise, of that first, hesitant discovery that comes just before the plunge into the gulf of I-think-I-love-her and she's-the-woman-of-my-life, that crucial moment when you choose between going for the one-night stand or the long haul. Let's be honest: between possession and abandonment. I made the same gesture with Isabelle at two in the morning in a bar filled with smoke, and not the kind that comes from tobacco. I felt death breathing down my neck, I was as desperate as my father is now, and I chose abandonment. I wish she were here now to tell me what to do with two old-timers giving themselves over to the same need.

William is no longer staring. Mother is trembling again. My father says he's hungry but doesn't let go of my mother's hand, and he repeats himself as though important words are stronger than dysfunctioning neurons.

"I'm hungry and I want a good death."

That's exactly how he says it, with maybe a slight hesitation before "I want a good death."

"We'll start with food, my husband. There's plenty of time for death later."

"No... I'm... tired... Die."

Is it possible that my mother finally feels free? She gets up and, laughing, recounts how we wanted to kill him by stuffing him with bacon, foie gras, pig's knuckles, beef marrow, Saint-Nectaire and wine. My father sputters and laughs. "Great idea!" he manages to stammer. William adds timidly that she forgot the baked ham and Chinese take-outs. We laugh openly, almost gaily. My mother brings in a bottle of wine. She opens the fridge and takes out salads, greens, red and orange peppers, fruit, cartons of soy milk and vegetarian hamburgers to reveal her secret stash in the back: Camembert, sliced garlic sausage, a small pot of goose rillettes, a thick slice of coarse pâté. She makes no excuses for having hidden these forbidden delicacies. She confesses it openly, asking only that we keep it to ourselves. She believed in all the diets, the medical injunctions, the regimens imposed on my father, who really did look sickly. But not for herself, who was living as close to death as he was. She doled out a little to him from time to time, when he begged and pleaded, the way one gives a child the candy that is normally denied him. But not too much. She was afraid of being caught by her children. Maybe they knew more about keeping an old man alive than she did. In short, she didn't want to hurt us.

"You...cheated!"

"Yes...for a long time. Ever since your stroke. I wanted to keep you around."

"Bread! Butter!"

He makes short work of a butter-and-rillettes tartine, drains his glass of wine in three gulps and asks for more. William tells him he's eating too fast, he could choke and die. Then he takes it back, realizing you can't accuse someone of chasing after death when you've just handed him death on a plate. My father is eating fast for our sake, making sure there won't be any death left for the rest of us. But he agrees to slow down. He takes a slice of bread, spreads butter on it, piles on five slices of garlic sausage and hands it to my mother with his toothless, timid baby's grin.

The Dictator is free. He has no more orders. He can only ask and give.

"It's good."

"Yes, very good."

It's not a statement, but rather a question seeking approval and thanks. It's a conversation.

"I'd like another one."

My mother has never asked my father for anything. She interceded on our behalf, tried to make the punishment not quite so violent. But for herself she made do. She never said, Pass the salt, or, I'd like another slice of ham. If she wanted salt it was there on the table, where she had put it. The ham was sliced, all she had to do was make up the children's plates and then her own. All my father ever did was eat.

"Not... good... for... you... Wine?"

Another question. My mother smiles. Yes, with pleasure. His hand shakes, the bottle wavers, wine trickles into her glass and some of it spills onto the table. William takes the bottle and says he wants a glass, too. My father laughs and makes another sandwich for my mother, then takes a heel of bread and dips it in the wine that has pooled on the table. Chin-chin, says Mother. There's another bottle in the cupboard behind the pasta. Nervously, William pours himself some wine; some goes on the table, some in his glass.

"Park... in... son's... William..."

And my father wipes up more wine with his bread. "This my body... this my blood," he says, and swallows Christ whole. My mother laughs. She'd forgotten, she says, that her husband had a sense of humour.

"When I first met your father he always made me laugh. Do you remember how funny you were?"

"Yes."

We hear the front door open and the Banker appears in the doorway. Visits from the children have become more frequent in the past year, and come at the most unexpected times. We invent reasons for dropping in, excuses my mother is not taken in by, but she doesn't mind. The children are keeping an eye on them, because of my father's falls, because his illness is becoming more and more worrisome, because my mother is exhausted. And anyway, these short visits break the silence, which for her is not the absence of sound, but the absence of conversation. I believe she has survived so well because she can still talk.

"So, I see we're ignoring all the advice from the doctors. I was bringing you some salad and a bowl of basmati rice."

She is angry. It's quite obvious. Her eyes accuse my mother of treason. And William, drinking wine. My mother replies calmly that we're just finishing up the leftovers from Christmas dinner, that it still feels a bit like Christmas.

"Sal...ad...Yuck."

And my father grabs the wine bottle and hands it to the Banker, who winces and shoots us a vicious look.

"You're completely drunk and ridiculous. Mother, we'll talk about this later. As for you," she says, looking at my father, "you are obviously trying to kill yourself."

She doesn't hear his Yes because it's muffled by a mouthful of pâté and bread. Like a vaudeville actress, she tosses her head, hoists her enormous bosom with her crossed arms and stomps out. My father laughs. My mother's expression is veiled. William pours himself a bit more wine. I'm relieved. With the intrusion and another round of wine after William digs out the second bottle, the conversation might get stalled. We'll talk about the Banker for a while, my father will fall asleep, my mother's eyes will flutter and she'll talk about going to bed. William, who has been drinking too fast, will get the hiccups, and we'll settle on a date for another get-together over veal liver and lobster and steak tartare with fries after all the entrées we can possibly eat. And then, of course, the cheeses: the raw-milk Bries, the triple-creams, the Pont-l'Évêque; followed by tarte tatin with ice cream. Did I forget to mention the beef marrow and the escargot Chablisienne, the pig's knuckles and the eggs in red wine sauce? I hope to stuff them both with enough fat to plug every artery in their bodies, to thicken their blood to the point of coagulation, let it bring on a stroke or a bout of terminal indigestion. I'm ready to help them die a natural death, maybe accelerate the aging process by drowning them in glucose and calories, but not to kill them, even if they ask me to. I have no desire to be an assassin. I know, I know, it wouldn't be murder, it would be called euthanasia. I'm in favour of euthanasia, I've signed a petition calling for it, I've brought up Holland as an example of a society motivated by compassion. But it is not in me to kill my parents. And yet I hope...

"Grandma, how do you want to die?"

"Asleep in my bed, like anyone else."

"Yeah."

"Except that I think, given where we are at this moment, with your grandfather and me it's a bit different. Dying in bed, in your sleep, that's what people hope for if they're afraid of dying. When you're afraid of dying it makes sense that you don't want to be aware you're dying at the moment it happens. With us, we want to decide when it's time, we want to have time to say goodbye, to have a look around, to do things we like doing. For example, I'd like to go to France before I die. There, you see, I'd forgotten about it because your grandfather couldn't go with me. Do you understand? To do a few wonderful things, then come home, go to bed, look at the wall at the end of the bed one last time, the photographs on the bedside table, and then just drift off to sleep thinking okay, that's it, I'm too tired to wake up and I've done everything I wanted to do down here. Knowing that when you close your eyes you enter the end of your life. You know, I'm talking calmly about it now, but I admit I'm a bit afraid. It's like diving into a lake for the first time. I'm not afraid of dying, but I am afraid of what happens after that."

She has been speaking quietly, almost in a whisper, as though she were telling a story to a child who was going to sleep. My father nods his agreement and pours a glass of wine. She turns to me.

"You must know Dr. Death, the American."

Yes, I know about Jack Kevorkian. A dozen or so years ago I thought of writing a play loosely based on his story. At first, only hopeless cases go to him, people with terminal illnesses or debilitating diseases like Alzheimer's or sclerosis of the liver. Those are the first 138 people he helps to commit suicide. In my play, he starts thinking of himself as God. He calls himself the Medical Liberator. He's a marketing genius, taking out huge ads on television and radio. You are exhausted by life, you want to die, but you don't have the courage to do it alone. Well, I'm here to free you from your intolerable burden. Professional treatment, satisfaction guaranteed. In my play, the *deus ex machina* doesn't ask if his client is bipolar, and so he doesn't prescribe lithium. As Dr. Life, he opens Houses of Death, welcoming, functioning hospices, just as we are in the process of opening Houses of Life. Where we have midwives helping people give birth, he has midwives helping people to die. In my play, a young black girl walks onstage, hunched over, face covered with the marks of a brutal attack. She says a few words about how tired she is, how she's had enough. The doctor knows that she's been raped. He doesn't even ask. He imagines the shame, the rejection by her family, her precarious future as an unemployed single mother. He doesn't hesitate a second; he offers her a death room, free of charge. He can afford to be generous. This is where I stopped writing, because I was at the point where I had to ask the question: Can a person be mistaken in thinking he wants to die? I've read that thousands of women were raped in Rwanda and gave birth to their accursed children whose fathers were rapists and murderers, but my friend Esther has told me that many of those children are happy and that their mothers, although they certainly contemplated suicide, have gone on to mend their lives with the fragile branches of hope. So if we agree with people when they say they want to die, might we not be denying ourselves a few happy children? The question my play wanted to ask, I now know, is so complex I don't even have the words to phrase it. But I continue mulling it over as I watch my mother chatting with William, and my father spitting a mouthful of bread into his plate without my mother even furrowing her brow. If a person wants to die, you kill him. That's how you show respect for the wishes of another. That at least is the equation. But what if a person tells you he wants to die and he's wrong, he doesn't really want to die? He has exaggerated his suffering, wants only to be comforted, supported, someone to be a springboard, someone to give him something to help see him through. Because in heavy black boxes he has hidden the magnificent drawings that he has never shown anyone because his father always yelled at him, called him stupid for drawing frogs with the heads of birds and the eyes of little girls. If you kill him, you're a murderer, not a friend. Or take a more complicated example. Your mother, who all her life has been perfectly reasonable and sensible, asks you to kill her. You know how exhausted she is, even if you don't know anything about her private pain and humiliation. Out of compassion, you accept. But what if she's wrong? What if my father's wish to die is just another of his endless crises of pride? What if all either of them wants is a little more happiness in the short time that remains to them, time which they can feel seeping into their bones and arteries? So there it is, my answer. They want to die as quickly as possible, but they want to die happily and naturally. But what is happiness to the elderly who say they want to go?

I tell them the story of Dr. Kevorkian, who was sentenced to twenty-five years in prison for second-degree murder. I explain his modus operandi. A suicide machine was left on the patient's bedside table. The patient operated the mechanism, which first injected him with a powerful sleeping draft, and then, ten minutes later, with a lethal dose of potassium chloride. Death was guaranteed. In my research I also discovered a machine made by the Australian doctor Philip Nitschke. I don't know what this one looked like, but it emitted a litre of carbon monoxide per minute. Death came as a gentle form of intoxication. A congenial death! The victim was spared the tedious business of attaching some kind of tube, usually a rubber garden hose, to his or her car's tailpipe, and... well, you know the drill. We all know the problem of committing suicide in an automobile. The set-up is fairly simple plumbing, but it leaves the victim a lot of time to have second thoughts. My father and mother are too tired for that.

My mother doesn't like such a mechanical way of ending her life. William, on the other hand, thinks it would be cool to have some kind of contraption meting out death with scientific precision. If he knew the exact formula for the sleeping draft and the gas, he could make one of those machines. My mother asks him if he wants to end up in prison like the American doctor.

"A... good... death," my father says. "We... have... no... car."

My mother laughs.

"We could rent one," Sam laughs with her. "We could rig it up and start a business."

Dad laughs, everyone laughs. Sam beams with pleasure. He feels useful. He reaches his hand out to my father and, when my father's hand moves towards his he raises it, fingers spread wide, and waits. My father, who does almost nothing but watch television and so is familiar with the new customs of adolescent culture, instantly understands Sam's gesture, and also opens his palm and spreads his fingers. They give each other high-fives, which they repeat as though they were both members of the same gang.

"So what are we going to eat on New Year's Eve?" my mother asks.

From his backpack, Sam takes a piece of rolled paper tied with a red ribbon, which looks a bit like a diploma.

"Here's the other half of your Christmas present, Grandpa. It was supposed to go with the madiran. The Nicolas Web site also publishes recipes."

He hands the scroll to me and says: "Read it."

"'The true recipe for Cassoulet de Castlenaudary. In a large, earthenware casserole dish place a quarter of a litre of dried white beans that have been soaked in water for several hours, add 300 grams of salt pork belly, 200 grams of bacon, one carrot, one onion stuck with six cloves, and a bouquet garni containing three cloves of garlic. Cover with water and simmer until beans are soft.

"'In a frypan, fry until golden in lard or, preferably, goose fat, 750 grams of lean pork and 500 grams of lean lamb liberally seasoned with salt and pepper. When the meat is the desired colour, add two finely minced onions, a bouqet garni and two garlic cloves, crushed. Allow to simmer for about one hour, adding beef broth as needed to keep the mixture moist. A small amount of tomato paste or several peeled, diced tomatoes may also be added.'"

"Yes... tomatoes," my father says, almost without drawling, as though his Parkinson's is in remission.

He is not drooling, his mouth is watering. He wipes his lips with the back of his hand and holds his pewter wine cup with a steady hand.

"'When the beans are ready, remove the carrot, onion and bouquet garni and add the pork and lamb, pieces of fresh garlic-flavoured pork sausage, saucisson and goose confit. Simmer for one hour. Remove the pieces of meat. Cut the pork, lamb, sausages and goose into thin, equal slices. Line the bottom of an earthenware pot with slices of bacon and a bed of beans, then a layer of the sliced meat with the sauce, then more beans, then more meat, and so on, ending with thin slices of salt pork belly, bacon and sausage. Then sprinkle with bread crumbs and moisten with goose fat. Cover the pot and allow to bake in the oven at a low temperature for 90 minutes. Serve.'"

"Do you know where the word *cassoulet* comes from, Grandpa? It's an old word from Languedoc, a region in the southwest of France, and it comes from the word *cassoule,* which was the earthenware bowl that they simmered the stew in."

"I want some."

My father is not expressing a desire; for the first time in years he is issuing an order.

"Even... if... not... good for... my heart."

And he pounds his chest hard, just to the right of centre, where he thinks his heart is situated.

ISABELLE AMAZES ME. I TELL HER ABOUT OUR LUNCH, STILL CAUGHT UP IN MY CONFUSION BETWEEN DREAM AND REALITY, SURprised to find myself laughing about it, stunned at feeling close to this couple I have never really believed in and who now seem to be taking shape before my very eyes. You were laughing at death, she says, do you realize that? So what did you decide? Nothing, really, nothing specific. That's the whole problem. My father went to lie down and my mother ended the discussion by tossing the ball into our court with a malicious little smile, as though to say: "Now that you know what we want, what are you going to do to help us?" What she in fact said was that for New Year's Eve dinner we'll have the cassoulet, nothing else—oh, she almost forgot, oysters for appetizers. And cheese, of course, and why not a Saint-Honoré cake? As for the other thing, she said, simply, probably for my benefit, we'll talk about it later, when the time comes. There are a few things they have to do first. Like what? Oh, maybe go camping and fishing, we'll discuss it later, dear. And she showed us calmly to the door.

"You laughed at death?" Isabelle repeats, with a smile.

Well, yes, but not as much as they did, and Isabelle, you cannot imagine the storm of controversy that this menu of hers is going to unleash. I can hear the Homeopath, the Banker and the Nurse already, the scornful, nasty remarks they'll make every time my father takes a mouthful of food, the I-told-you-so's with every belch and hot flash. The New Year will begin with unbearable family chaos. So what's new? she says, putting her arms around me. According to her, I have the only totally dysfunctional family that seems to function very well, thank you very much, and keeps on functioning, albeit in a kind of chaotic harmony. This organized shambles, this cacophony of orders, opinions, directives and proclamations in which I have lived since childhood, doesn't really bother me. It's my mother and father who terrify me. Dad, knowing nothing of our wild machinations, and Mother, who knows my every thought, chose us, William-Sam and me, to be their Dr. Kevorkian. At a time to be determined by them, without consulting us, they'll tip us the nod and we'll off them. Because despite all the hilarity we have entered into a pact. Nothing stated, nothing so firm as a handshake, but a contract nonetheless. We know we said Yes. The word *yes* has been resounding in my head for a long time now, taking up all available space, swallowing neurons left and right, whether my mouth was able to articulate it or not. I have had the psychological equivalent of Parkinson's disease.

IT'S RAINING CATS AND DOGS. DECEMBER 31ST IN A YEAR OF GLOBAL WARMING. WHEN I ARRIVED WITH WILLIAM TO START THE CAS-soulet, my mother told me that there was nothing to worry about, all the children have been told what was on the menu and in each case their medical and moralistic jeremiads stopped when she explained to them that this would be their last New Year's Eve. The Banker, who's been cool with my mother since Boxing Day, comes into the kitchen chewing out her husband for not holding the umbrella properly and hands me a bag, saying she made a rice salad for anyone who still has a brain left in their head. "You're free to eat whatever you want, my dear," my mother tells her, "even in my house, but don't put it on the table. You can come in here to the kitchen to serve yourself."

"Mother, be reasonable."

"We'll talk about it tomorrow, dear."

Hardly anyone arrives empty-handed. It's as though habit has more weight with them than my mother's wishes. Each carries a dish, as tradition dictates, even though she told them all not to bring anything. She greets everyone by saying, "Thanks but no thanks." The Homeopath is practically in tears and my mother has to be firm. For lunch she and my father had calf's liver and bacon, English style. My sister, who calls herself a natural healer after having come out of a long depression and is now a rabid vegetarian and a fierce separatist, regards eating English calf's liver as an insult to nature and capitulation to the enemy.

After spending time in the kitchen pouring ourselves aperitifs, we move into the family room, lightly touching Dad's hand or kissing him gingerly on the lips, as we would a religious relic, without expecting an answer to our How-are-you-feelings. We've been like this since the onset of his illness. Mother has already been drinking. I tell her I can tell, smiling. A little port, dear, it gives me strength for the meal. William looks worried and his mother hugs him, happy that he's thinking about the two casseroles in the oven rather than the classic Russian Opening in chess. The tragedy of modern parenthood: they no longer have children, they have strangers in children's bodies. My mother interrupts my thoughts.

"Your father is writing now. He writes instead of trying to talk."

After we left on Boxing Day he sat down at his desk, took a pad of lined paper from the drawer and for hours forced himself to line up a series of letters, rapt in studious silence as though he had gone back to elementary school. First he covered an entire page with *a*'s, then *b*'s, right up to z's, the entire alphabet, then carefully placed the pages in the drawer as if they were a valuable document. The next day, more pages were covered with words, random and with no apparent sense connecting them—smoke, eat, thanks, slut, Europe—dozens and dozens of words settling themselves more or less comfortably on the lines of the paper. Then he started on sentences, most of which also had no meaning. "A butterfly cries bacon." When my mother asked him what it meant, he wrote: "Nothing. I'm just writing sentences that stay on the lines, and as you should know it's not easy to start speaking again. I try words. I put them together in a straight line." He spent the entire week working like an opinionated and persevering schoolboy. My mother had to go to a stationery store to buy another dozen pads of lined paper and some notebooks. For her it was a week of serene calm and happiness such as she had not known in three years. He wrote ceaselessly. That afternoon he handed her a page from a notebook. She crumpled it up and stuck it in her sleeve, as the absent-minded aged do with Kleenex. She smooths it out and hands it to me. The writing is shaky but clear. "It's a good idea to go together." Yes. A tear floods down a crease in her face. She does not wipe it away with the back of her hand, as she normally would do. It poises at the top of her lip, drops onto her tongue, and she licks it. A liberated tear, probably her first.

A strong smell coming from the oven is worrying Sam. It's burning. I assure him it's not. It's just the garlic and the lard and the tomato starting to fuse and percolate. Think of it as the beginning of the perfect cassoulet. Suddenly silence falls on the room. One of the brothers-in-law is saying something. "You all talk at the same time. No one listens to anyone. You behave like children. This is not how I raised you." He's reading a message my father has handed him.

We haven't forgotten his existence, since his existence has been the centre of our family life as a boil is the focal point of a face, making you forget the look or the smile. But we have forgotten that he can hear us, that he can think, that he is still alive. We've been in the presence of an animated dead man, a sort of out-of-order machine that nonetheless continues to emit sounds and move about in a disarticulated manner. And now the dead man has refound his voice and, even more troubling, has gone back to being the little father of the people. He hasn't changed. He is immutable. From the kitchen I watch him scribbling in his notebook. He writes with an anxious fury. I take in the sudden, jerking movements of the pen, the impatient erasures, the guttural sounds coming from deep in his chest. He rips the sheet from the notebook and gives it to my mother, who has come into the room for it. William says, "It's ready." Mother reads: "I am not sick. I am very old. You want to save me from dying. That's very kind. I want to die the way I want. I'm hungry. Shut up!"

The family is silent. The two casserole dishes are steaming on the table, along with four platters of oysters, cheese, a salad and a Saint-Honoré cake glistening in the room's light like a Tower of Babel defying God and all His prescriptions. My mother doesn't like oysters, I remember now, but she hides a grimace and says, "Good," as my father knocks them back like petits fours. All the children eat with their heads down, eyeing my father from the corners of their eyes to see what kind of mood he's in. *Canadian Idol* is on television, my father's favourite program; Wilfred, the favourite of grandmothers and nubile young things, is singing. My father scribbles something. "Pavarotti is better," my mother reads. A proclamation has been released. The conversation turns to opera, which no one likes, but we do like the Three Tenors.

Sam opens a bottle of old madiran and plays sommelier. My father doesn't realize that he's supposed to taste the wine and approve the choice, and we watch the ceremony, intrigued and surprised by it. Sam remains imperturbable, stays in his role, waiting. We have been waiting on my father for three years. We rarely ask his opinion unless it's in the form of an interrogative affirmation. He has been hospitalized in his own house and cared for by his own creatures. I think he has become accustomed to thinking of himself not as a client but as a beneficiary, obliged to accept the service that is so generously given for his gratification. The beneficiary doesn't refuse or criticize, he only thanks. Discountenanced, my father looks at his grandson with moist eyes, drinks the dribble of wine and says: "More." You approve of the wine, sir? says Sam. My father nods, Yes, and says, "More," and Sam fills his pewter cup almost to overflowing, which evokes from the Banker the comment that there is no need to ruin the Provençal tablecloth she gave Mother for her last anniversary. Sam continues serving, since this is his meal, his gift, which he imagines will be deliciously deadly. He stands stiff as a maître'd in a posh restaurant and places the best pieces of confit and sausage delicately on my father's plate. My father grabs the bread and spoons himself more beans. The plate is overflowing and my father looks anxiously at my mother, from whom he is used to hearing reprimands about his gourmandizing and his gluttony. She turns to Sam and says, smiling, "Sam, you certainly know how to serve grandfathers, but grandmothers are a little more fragile. I want a bit of everything, but not as much as my husband." Eyes widen around the table. Grumbling is heard. My father raises his pewter cup and gives a toast that none of us understand. Several of us lift our glasses mechanically. The silence that falls on the cassoulet eaters is broken only by my father's intestinal rumblings and belches. He eats as though he is expecting to die in the next few minutes. My mother puts a hand on his, the one holding the fork, and asks him if he would like a napkin. Yes, all right, says his head, that is what he seems to want. A napkin, which my mother places in his hand and which he raises to his dripping lips. I watch him, and he doesn't notice that I am observing him as closely as a doctor observes the symptoms of a patient in the terminal phase of illness. He eats like a man trying to wolf down his life. With a sense of joyous urgency.

The Banker and her husband are arguing. He reaches for the cassoulet, passing on the basmati rice with rice vinegar dressing and garnished with sprigs of Italian parsley that she has placed in front of them. The Homeopath gets up to fetch the raw vegetables with which she hopes to break up all the trans fats she has unenthusiastically introduced into her bloodstream. Her polite husband does not insist. The Tragedienne bursts out laughing and congratulates her son on his cassoulet, which she says is like manna from heaven. My mother doesn't hear her. She is eating. My father is not listening. He is elsewhere, in the casserole that is soon going to be empty, and maybe he'll ask someone to give him some cheese and chocolate mousse. The Banker is finding it intolerable that her husband thinks for one minute that she prefers some regimen to her own father. He thinks she does. The Banker is having trouble breathing. She is trying to swallow her pride and it isn't going down well. In fact, she's choking on it. The man with whom she has been living for more than twenty years stands up without looking at her.

"I'm going to sleep in a hotel. I'll come and collect my things in the morning."

"You can't do this to me in front of everyone!"

She doesn't sound sad, simply irritated. As if by magic her breathing returns to normal. Isabelle tells me to do something. There's nothing to do, as my mother understands. She continues nibbling at a duck drumstick, unperturbed. My father writes and hands me the notebook. "Is he really going to a hotel?" I think so, yes. He smiles broadly and makes a grab for the bread.

The Geographer has rounded up his three children, who don't want to leave before dessert. He loses his temper and roughly grabs the oldest child's elbow, and the child howls in pain. The Homeopath protests this display of violence. The father bridles at the intrusion into his private domain and advises the Homeopath to confine herself to educating her own two sons, who have already tried to get his oldest to smoke pot. The Homeopath's two sons protest loudly. My sister is seized with doubt and horror by the thought that she has brought her boys up badly. Her husband says: "Calm down, they've been smoking up for a long time."

"Oh, come on, it's no big deal."

I don't know what I'm doing, standing here trying to calm everyone down. The Tragedienne asks Sam if he's smoking marijuana, too, and is reassured by his declaration that pot and chess don't go well together.

Of course they all turn on me. "What's it to you, you who have always kept your distance, you who don't believe in the family and always look down your nose at us?" They're not entirely wrong, but they're not right, either. I do not look down my nose at them, but I do try to keep my distance. And by having been forced into attending these family gatherings, I've learned to love my family. All the same, I refuse to fall for the old family mystique. The family is a fragile construction in which each member looks for a strength he lacks on his own. It's also a political invention, a kind of political party that couldn't survive without compromises and falsehoods. They're right: why am I getting involved? They're the ones jostling for position in the family party, not me. I gave when I had something to give, took when they had something I needed. I'm not saying I was devoid of affection, quite the contrary. You can't be this intimate with a group of men and women without loving them a little, perhaps even a lot, because families are so transparent. They strip us naked before our likenesses and our equals.

My mother raises her voice to explain that I've secretly been a big help. She exaggerates. I've done so little. But since it's the mother who invents the family, she has to defend its usefulness. And let's be frank: my mother needs this family to be united. Without that, she would have lived for nothing.

"You're all mental cases. You don't understand a thing. Grandpa and Grandma want to die, and me and my uncle are looking for ways to help them."

Sam goes back to his cassoulet. His mother chokes, horrified. Silence drops like a lead balloon. My mother says nothing. My father asks for some bread for his Pont-l'Évêque. The Geographer tells his children to go play in the yard and they say it's pouring rain. My mother asks for some wine. The Nurse says to Sam's mother that there must be some misunderstanding, and Sam's mother looks at Sam, who says, No, there is no misunderstanding. They only have to ask Grandma and Grandpa.

Silence. A very long silence.

"My husband and I don't want to go on living. For me life has become a trial. For him, it's more like an obligation. So we've told ourselves that we should die happy as quickly as possible rather than go on living because we're obliged to."

Liquid is trickling from my father's nose and mouth. He looks happy.

My mother is no longer shrinking.

"Cassoulet!"

My mother's words and my father's approving grunts do not have the desired effect. The meal ends with a clinking of utensils and Pass the salt, rather than with the usual babbling and outbursts of conversation. The farewell kisses are polite, the See you laters few, despite Mother's radiant smile and my father's almost indecent joy.

■　　■　　■

IT IS ALMOST APRIL AND THERE ARE DARK RIVULETS RUNNING THROUGH THE SNOW IN FRONT OF THE HOUSE. PATCHES OF LAWN APPEAR here and there, giving off the slightly sour odour of putrefaction that signifies rebirth. Sam and I have continued our project of gastronomical murder, but without much expectation of success. We go to the house once or twice a week, carrying plates of prepared food, and sometimes we stay and cook. Today it'll be calf's liver à la Venitienne. But the family is no longer the same. When we celebrate birthdays there is always someone missing, and those who are there complain that the food is too heavy. My father communicates more and more by writing, which leaves less time for the rest of us to talk. He reiterates his moderately racist phobias, tells his bad jokes about homosexuals and artists like me who do nothing useful with our lives. And he has gone back to giving orders, via the written word. In private, one of us says that he was better when he wasn't so alive, so present. In other words, Stalin's return hasn't pleased anyone except my mother.

The Banker saw her husband again for only thirty minutes. The morning after the dinner, when he came to collect his clothes and left without saying goodbye. He must be sleeping with his secretary, why else would he not answer any of her questions? The Homeopath and her husband aren't getting along well, either. He's in favour of euthanasia. The Geographer doesn't bring his children when he comes, which is seldom. And the Tragedienne is paying for her son's frankness. Two sisters now hold her responsible for the whole drama. If only your son played sports.

"You and Sam haven't asked me a single question since we told you we wanted to die."

My mother dips her bread in gravy as thick as melted chocolate. I'm very pleased with this gravy, she says. I think I finally got it right. She laughs, watching my father stuff his face, but I don't follow up on her first comment, which brings back the anguish I feel every time I think of this pact that I'm not at all certain I have concluded.

"I have some bad news. My husband passed all his tests yesterday and the doctor says he no longer needs to take them. He's getting better."

Rigid Parkinson's is characterized by irreversible degeneration. An irregular but constant downward curve. She takes the pen and my father's notebook and traces a descending line that levels out and then turns upwards. He grunts with pleasure.

"Since... eating... less... sick."

"I told the doctor that since he's been happier he's been

less sick. The doctor said it's either a statistical error or else a false remission."

Sam, who is more innocent than I am, and therefore more courageous, asks if that means they no longer want to die.

"No, Sam, dear. We don't know how we're going to decide to die, but we're certain it will be soon. But first my husband and I want to do one thing: go camping again, go on a fishing trip to the Baskatong Reservoir."

My father, who was obviously waiting for that phrase, opens his notebook. "And I'll steal the biggest walleye from you." He has been rehearsing his response.

I know it is stupid to remember a stolen walleye after fifty years, a chintzy trophy, a cup no more than twenty centimetres high, an object of surpassing ugliness with a vaguely fish-like, though not walleye-like, shape to it and an inscription engraved on the base: "Thousand Island River, 1950, Molson Walleye Derby." I've never once won first prize in anything, always either an honourable mention or sometimes no mention at all, not even when I thought I ought to have been.

I really wish now that he would give me permission to kill him. I wouldn't do it for his sake, but I'd do it for mine. And for my mother's. To kill someone you have to either love them or hate them. I've never been able to love him, and now with his illness I can't hate him. We're back at square one. Images and shouts crowd around each other. I don't know if it's my mother who is crying or me. I remember standing up to Stalin, throwing some object or other at his face, I remember my revolt surprising him so much that he didn't retaliate, so astonished was he at the rebellion of his people, a rebellion he had not imagined possible. My mother moved to protect me from a blow that never came. She ordered me to go to my room. But it was you I was defending, Mother. Why are you punishing me? From that day on I knew I did not love my father. More than that, from that day on I have not understood my relationship with my mother, who did not stand up for me. I do not understand her resignation, unless it is to be found in those photos, that novel-in-photographs of her life. Freedom, perhaps, revolt, the price of her revolution. The change in her life, the hopes, the reality and finally the silence and the feeling of having dared something, which confers a sense of pride and allows her to at least have memories of heroism. My mother's story is the story of Cuba. My father, Stalin, Castro, the same battle. Such dreams, so beautiful, and so betrayed. These are the worst memories, the most persistent. How can one rebel against one's liberators? In fact, I reproach my mother for still loving my father, and I reproach my father for not having loved her more. There it is, the dilemma all children face: to understand why parents, whom we do not love equally, find themselves at the end of their lives, obligatory accomplices to be sure, but lovers nonetheless. And to come to the obligation of loving them ourselves. Yes, to love them, forgetting our whole previous lives. Our parents are not just our mothers and our fathers, they are also human beings, and human beings die. Painful memories are erased.

I REMEMBER NOW. The oldest rock, the one from the Canadian Shield, which carried within itself all the secrets of the Ice Ages, of climate changes, and Lake Iroquois, where my city, Montreal, is now, where I first heard Bach's toccatas and ate my first piece of stinking cheese and learned my fastidious lessons about beavers and mushrooms and Nat King Cole, who led me to Brubeck and then to Coltrane. The books he read and that I read after him, in secret. The desire to know everything to be able to talk about everything. The refusal to conform to dress codes and that totally brutal frankness. All of that was simply a way of teaching, ordering, forbidding in my child's head, obligatory lessons, shameful lessons, perhaps, humiliating, often, but maybe that was how I came to discover the universe, how I became curious and perhaps an artist and also proud and broken, as one of my sisters sometimes scolded me for. I was not born of his violence, but rather from that first rock picked up on a path that led to our being lost. I did not love my father, but I have a father. And I am glad of that.

I'D FORGOTTEN HOW MONOTONOUS THE
HIGHWAY IS NORTH OF SAINT-JOVITE, HOW
UGLY THE HUMAN-CONSTRUCTED COUNTRYSIDE
can be. My father is grumbling because I'm driving too
slowly for him. But my ancient Volvo has never pulled a
trailer before, especially one whose axle is probably rusty
from not having been used for ten years. My mother sold
the car, afraid of being killed at an intersection because my
father insisted on driving despite the trembling in his
hands and his irregular heartbeat, but she never once con-
sidered getting rid of the trailer. It was in this scrap heap
that, in the sixties, she discovered the Rocky Mountains
and saw the Pacific Ocean from Vancouver. A cross-Canada
trip that still makes her eyes light up when she talks about
it. And so we have this little trailer, a relic from another
age, a gypsy caravan, as though my mother and father
belonged to the age of explorers, this trailer that my father
saw every day in the garage and which made him feel that
maybe one day he'd go on another camping trip. The thing

also took them to New Brunswick and Newfoundland. We know nothing about those times except from the photos that show only my mother. We never wondered how they were able to spend so much time together when we assumed they didn't love each other. My father murmurs "Nominingue," and my mother explains that that they used to buy bum bread in this village, traditional loaves that my father was so fond of he always stocked up on them when we went fishing in the Baskatong Reservoir. The smell of almost burnt toast suddenly comes to me, along with the perfume of warm spruce needles, and my father's good mood brought on by thick slices of bread dripping with butter. Sam is tapping on the back of my seat in time to the electro-acoustic music he listens to. There is no longer a bakery in Nominingue. We find some imitation bum bread in Mont-Laurier.

Since my father's health has improved, and he eats whatever he wants, and my mother has learned all our recipes, and the doctors scratch their heads over this Parkinson's remission, William, also known as Sam, and I no longer know what role we're supposed to be playing. Sam swore to me that his grandmother's cassoulet was better than his own, more unctuous, he said, and I marvelled that a teenager would know that word. He was offended. We're friends again now because we share this terrible secret, the imminent death of my father and my mother. I wonder if they brought sleeping pills with them and if they'll commit suicide in the trailer while Sam and I are asleep in the tent, since he and I have chosen to freeze to death in the tent rather than cohabit uneasily in the trailer. Preoccupied by these thoughts, I drive somewhat erratically, and my father complains. Of course he would rather be driving himself. We're taking him home. My mother is humming a tune to herself.

For my father, the Baskatong was the Kenya for safari lovers of the 1950s. Rhinoceroses and lions guaranteed. This immense reservoir formed by the construction of a bridge by a paper company harboured huge lake trout and enormous pike. Only serious fishermen came here, those more in quest of trophies they could display than of fish they could eat. As I recall, we had only partial success. Pike weighing a few kilos, but never the lake trout that lurked a hundred metres below the surface and could wrench the pole from your hands.

It's three in the afternoon when we arrive. We've been driving for six hours and my mother suggests we eat. She has made canapés and gizzard salad. Sam busies himself putting up the tent, a small blue dome that he sets up on a mound of moss still yellow from the winter. It's the 20th of May but there is still a bit of ice in the water. My father is sitting in his wheelchair, looking out over his lake.

"Now. Fish."

The two words came out smoothly, without hesitation, perfectly formed. They are an injunction, an order. Sam has already taken the poles and tackle box out of the trailer. He, too, wants to get out on the water and catch a fish, which he has never done. My father explains hesitantly but clearly about spinners and lines, leads and hooks. Sam tries a few casts, a precise and attentive pupil. My mother smiles and tells me they haven't yet decided when they will die but it won't be far off, and that they have all the sleeping pills they need. Is there something we can do? Yes, you can let us do it.

Proud as punch, my father sits enthroned like a king in his wheelchair in the centre of the boat. Sam is in the stern, steering the outboard motor according to my father's instructions. My mother sits in the bow, trailing her line in the water. I'm amidships. Mother asks me why I'm not fishing. I let my line fall into the lake. We drift on the gentle waves, little shivers of water. My mother's smile tenses. "A bite!" my father cries, and laughs. He makes fun of my mother. "Useless!" Mother, who knows nothing about fishing, reacts instinctively by jerking her pole up. It bends ominously. At the same moment my own line is yanked down into the depths. My mother becomes slightly excited. My father laughs even more. Mother's pole bends more sharply and she panics. She hands it to me. I know, I can sense, that at the end of my line is an enormous fish, a trophy like the one my father spirited away from me, a lake trout that haunts the depths of the lake. I need both hands, and my father laughs at our mutual disarray. My mother loses her pole. I grab it as my fish pulls me towards the bow. I am now holding two poles, each now obviously having hooked an enormous fish. Sam is jumping with excitement.

My father is still laughing. My fish pauses, trying to trick me, but I don't know that. Here, Dad, take my pole. He stands partway up, takes the pole in both hands and tries to set the hook. Big, he says, and in the deep, dark water a lake trout gives a sudden powerful pull. Dad! Grandpa!

He's already out of sight. I don't know how to swim, I explain to Sam. Then I turn to my mother, who gives a timid smile and takes my hand.

"Push me," she says.